JOHN JESURUN

Deep Sleep
White Water
Black Maria

A MEDIA TRILOGY

<u>NoPassport Press</u>
Dreaming the Americas Series

John Jesurun: Deep Sleep, White Water, Black Maria – A Media Trilogy
Copyright 2009, 1987, 1986 by John Jesurun.
"Introduction: Language Makes Itself Come True" copyright 2009 by Fiona Templeton.

NoPassport Press
Dreaming the Americas Series
First edition 2009 by NoPassport Press
PO Box 1786, South Gate, CA 90280 USA; -
NoPassportPress@aol.com
ISBN: 978-0-578-02602-2

Contents

Language Makes Itself Come True

If you've once seen a John Jesurun play that's how you read them. Fast. A Jesurun fan likes adrenalin; attention to detail. Things have got to get done before things change.

Yet all time is potentially present. In *Chang in a Void Moon*, John's Monday-night serial play at New York's Pyramid Club in the 80s, characters from multiple time periods and places in history interact with, exchange with and affect each other. It is as if characters and plots from every movie he'd seen or book he'd read or anything that had made him curious, latently inhabited the same space. But the characters were new, distillations. His culture is hybrid – Jesuits, spies, car mechanics, characters who speak only Spanish, saboteurs, a chair that plays the Infanta, Germans playing French, Native American arrows, lines from pop songs used straight as if they are our language (and they are). And his/our culture IS the real. The character of Chang was played by two people, visual opposites in the same costume (John Hagan and Donna Hermann), sometimes simultaneously, and even argued; dead characters returned, for after all they remained characters in the space-time continuum that warped just as *Chang* was a vast universe of plots whose tentacles extended endlessly extended in any direction. The more episodes there were, the harder John's task of introduction became to tell the story so far.

But it was his sets that kept this sprawling baroque in line. Like camera angles in film noir, the audience would be presented with different views of the same situation – from the sides, from above, as performers scrambled during the briefest of blackouts to move the rectangle of foam-core that was the table. The props were gestures (like the ice cubes that I held, as the blind king's blind daughter, that represented diamonds; but they were also ice cubes, as the diamonds miraculously melted).

It's hard to read and imagine the technical setups in John's productions – they are conceived by a profoundly 4-dimensional theatrical imagination. John thinks the whole space. Projection is not a gimmick, it is place inside place, it is in dialogue with the characters, it is our life with screens, it is a layer in the spectrum on which also sit audience and live performer, it is prior and future and present existence simultaneously. Watching *Deep Sleep* was like being IN *Deep Sleep*. It is how we speak in forked tongues. Or it is simply a pool. Or a white rectangle.

Nobody moves much in John's work, or perhaps, like Steve Buscemi's constant circling on a rope in *Shatterhand Massacree* at St Mark's Church, they are caught in a movement. They don't have to move much. The words are the action.

And all could be achingly deadpan funny, and all could be moving or frightening, and all could be instantly deflated. And all are followed breathlessly, wait, didn't she just say…

The interrogation of *White Water* is familiar territory in his plays – see also the start of *Deep Sleep* and of *Black Maria*. People want to know something, demand, repeat demands. There are

authorities, summits, religions, states, corporations
– the stakes are high, sanity is fluid, the human risks
itself, erupting through the oppression of control,
and those who are in control tumble suddenly.
Mack in *White Water* insists he telling the truth
about the one thing they want to know – not really
what happened but whether he is telling the truth –
but the slipperiness of his other facts goes by
unnoticed, like where his parents are – one moment
dead, the next in Tibet. There is often this second
register that is played at the highest points, or a
third or fourth or more – the fact that the mention of
Buchenwald is followed in *Number Minus One* by
the words of a Beatles song make it no less
important and neither less part of the fabric of the
world – on the contrary, the lyrics take on new
meaning.

John Jesurun's verbal images pile on each other,
cancel each other, are gorgeously evocative,
terrifyingly direct, disgustingly familiar,
apocalyptic. In his language all is possible (yes,
you CAN say that.) As in *White Water*, language
makes itself come true. For me John is a great poet
among modern playwrights. But, acting-wise, the
language is never milked (anyway there isn't time).
It abhors assumption, it has the best insults ever.

In much of his work, death is a major presence. In
Philoktetes, as in *Black Maria*, and in *Number
Minus One,* it is rubbed shoulders with, looked at in
its ugliest, and smelled at its sweetest – in
Whitewater the dead dog smells of flowers. The
passage that migrated to open *Philoktetes:*

Listen to me, I'm telling you something.
So that you'll learn the value of
suffering. The joy of sacrifice and
patience, murder and manslaughter. So
that you'll learn to speak the language
of the dead. Once again it's time for you
to shut up. Belly up to the buzzsaw.
gravitational collapse, Blackleg, Yankee
pot roast. Stop crying. You should be
happy. Listen to me, I'm telling you
something. You tell someone else and
they'll tell someone else. This is what
Philoktetes told me. This is his suicide
note, his poison-pen letter. First, I'll
give the clue, then the story, then the
real story. First what they saw, then
what was seen, then what was. The
cadaver will direct the autopsy, a
talking corpse narrating. A dead horse
talking, a dead foot walking.
Philoktetes is dead.

may be the most breathtaking opening to any play I
know. This was the 80s, when AIDS brought
crashing a generation of imaginations, people we
loved. And *Philoktetes* was performed again
recently, now when our hands are dirty with the
world's blood.

What's simple is complex and what's complex is
simple.

Fiona Templeton
January 2009

DEEP SLEEP

Photo credit: Massimo Agus.

DEEP SLEEP

Deep Sleep was first performed at the La
Mama ETC Annex in New York City on
February 1, 1986 with the following cast:

Whitey	Steve Buscemi
Emily	Valerie Charles
Bronski	Larry Tighe
Manitas	Sanghi Wagner
Sparky	Michael Tighe
Bodine	Black-Eyed Susan
Smith	John Hagan
Miranda	Annie Labois
Lee	Robyn Hatcher

Director- John Jesurun
Lighting Design: Jeff Nash
Technical Director: Jim Coleman
Camera/Line Producer: Richard Connors
Edit: John Jesurun, Richard Connors
Stage Manager: Brad Philips

This play was first published in *Wordplays 5*
PAJ Publications - 1986
ISBN: 1-55554-006-6 (cloth)
ISBN: 1-55554-007-4

Re-printed in this collection by permission of
PAJ and Bonnie Marranca.

The audience sits on both long sides of the rectangular playing space.

At the center of each end of the playing floor is a large clear plexiglass box, five feet high. Each box contains a 16mm film projector. Both projectors face each other and remain on throughout the performance. Behind each projector, six feet from the ground is a large screen, twenty-one feet high by twenty-eight feet wide. Images from the projectors will be received by these two screens. Four identical three ft. by three ft. tables. One at the center of the space, another one in a corner and the remaining two each positioned in front of one of the projectors. There is a large three by six mirror topped table on one side of the space opposite the center table. Each table is accompanied by one or two office chairs. On each table: a plate and eating utensils, ashtray. On SPARKY's table is constantly revolving record turntable, a record album and a bread roll. On one of the chairs at the center table is a clothed wooden puppet. On the center table, a bread roll.

SPARKY, nine years old in leather knickers sits at the corner table. EMILY sits at the table in front of the projector nearest him. Her chair is blue, her dress is blue, she wears a long black leather coat. BRONSKI sits at the center table in a dark business suit. MANITAS sits in front of the other projector in pants and a denim jacket. Except for SPARKY the live performers smoke almost continuously throughout the performance.

BOLD FACE LETTERS INDICATE WORDS AND ACTION FOR SCREEN PERFORMERS.

Live actors enter and take positions. Projectors begin in darkness on a dark stage.

Screen A and B: Twenty seconds of a passenger's point of view of a roller coaster ride.

CUT

Screen A: Extreme close-up of WHITEY's face moving slowly across the screen. (Thirteen seconds)

Screen B (Simultaneously) Extreme close-up of WHITEY's eye. This shot zooms out to reveal his full face. (Thirty seconds.)

CUT

SCREEN A: Wide shot, seated around a blue topped table are WHITEY in a red shirt, LEE in blue, BODINE in red and MIRANDA in black. SMITH, wearing a dark suit, stands behind them. Whitey is younger than the others on the screen. He wears a red shirt. His hair is white. The scene is viewed from a very high angle. When the actors address those on the stage they look up.

SCREEN B: A large window covers the screen. Through it is seen a blue sky. A translucent curtain is gently moving in the wind.

LEE: Good morning.
BODINE: Sorry I'm late, I couldn't find a place to park my car.
SMITH: That's alright.
MIRANDA: I didn't know you had a car.
BODINE: I just bought one.
SMITH: How's your daughter?
BODINE: She's fine. How are you, Whitey?
SMITH: Whitey.
MIRANDA: Sit down.
LEE: This is…who is this?
WHITEY: Oh…
MIRANDA: Who is this? You know who it is.
SMITH: This is our friend Miranda.
WHITEY: Miranda.
LEE: Now, let's see if you can close your eyes.
SMITH: Close your eyes.
MIRANDA: That's right, close them.

BODINE: What color do you see?
WHITEY: I don't.
LEE: What color do you see?
WHITEY: Blue.
BODINE: What kind of blue?
LEE: What kind?
SMITH: Sky blue, sea blue, cerulean blue, cobalt blue?
WHITEY: Prussian blue.
SMITH: Prussian blue.
LEE: Is it nice?
WHITEY: Yeah.
BODINE: Take this hand. (She offers her hand to Whitey.)
WHITEY: (Takes BODINE's hand) Whose hand is it?
BODINE: It's Bodine's hand.
SMITH: Right, and who is Bodine?
WHITEY: Bodine is my friend.
MIRANDA: What color do you see?
WHITEY: Blue, light blue.
MIRANDA: That's right.
LEE: Now, is that the color you want to see or the color we want to see?
WHITEY: It's the color I want to see.
BODINE: What else do you see?
WHITEY: I see an angel face. It's on top of an angel food cake and it is my own face and my own cake and Pinry is there too.
SPARKY: Whitey.
SMITH: Who's that?

SPARKY: Whitey.

LEE: Who's that?

SPARKY: It's me. Sparky.

WHITEY: Sparky?

BODINE: You know Sparky, your friend Sparky. He was on the roller coaster ride when you fell off.

WHITEY: I flew off. Is my doll there?

LEE: Pinry?

MIRANDA: Pinry.

WHITEY: Yes.

SPARKY: Whitey, it's me.

WHITEY: Who's that?

SPARKY: It's me. Sparky.

WHITEY: Hi, Sparky.

BODINE: Where's Sparky?

SMITH: He's here in this room.

BODINE: And what is your name?

WHITEY: What is my name? My name is Sparky.

SMITH: Your name is not Sparky.

WHITEY: What is my name?

BODINE: You know your name. What is your name?

WHITEY: I don't have a name.

LEE: You have a name.

WHITEY: I don't know my name. What is my name?

SMITH: You know you have a name.

WHITEY: I know I have a name.

MIRANDA: And what is that name?

WHITEY: That name is Sparky.

MIRANDA: No, Sparky is over there.

WHITEY: What is my name?

SMITH: You know your name.

WHITEY: What is my name?

SMITH: You know your name.

LEE: Sparky is over there.

WHITEY: My name is Sparky.

LEE: Sparky is not your name, Sparky is over there.

MIRANDA: Do you see Sparky?

WHITEY: I see Sparky.

SMITH: Do you see Sparky?

WHITEY: I see Sparky.

BODINE: Then what is your name?

WHITEY: My name is Sparky.

BODINE: Your name is not Sparky.

WHITEY: My name is not Sparky.

LEE: What is your name?

WHITEY: Then what is your name? I don't know.

BODINE: What is my name? My name is Bodine.

WHITEY: Your name is Bodine.

BODINE: Right, my name is Bodine.

MIRANDA: And my name is...?

WHITEY: Sparky.

MIRANDA: My name is not Sparky.

SPARKY: I'm Sparky.

WHITEY: You are Sparky.

SMITH: And who is that?

WHITEY: That is Lee.
BODINE: That is Lee.
LEE: And who is that?
WHITEY: That is Smith.
LEE: Right, that is Smith.
WHITEY: And that is Whitey.
LEE: No, you are Whitey.
WHITEY: I am Whitey.
SMITH: Your name is Whitey.
WHITEY: My name is Sparky.
BODINE: That is Sparky. You just said that your name is Whitey.
WHITEY: My name is Whitey Sparky.
EMILY: Your name is Whitey.
WHITEY: My name is Whitey.
LEE: Your name is Whitey.
WHITEY: My name is Whitey?
MIRANDA: There you are. What is your name?
WHITEY: My name is Sparky.
MIRANDA: Your name is not Sparky, your name is Whitey.
SPARKY: Why don't we just switch names?
SMITH: Because he must learn his name.
EMILY: Not with his brain in that condition.
SPARKY: What condition?
BODINE: You know what condition it is.
WHITEY: I don't want to talk about that now.
SPARKY: Whitey.
WHITEY: Sparky.
EMILY: Whitey.

BODINE: Let's not talk about it now.

WHITEY: And don't think I don't remember what happened.

MANITAS: We know you remember what happened.

WHITEY: And don't try to hide it from me.

SMITH: No one is trying to hide anything.

WHITEY: Yes, you are. Yes, you are.

LEE: We are not, Whitey.

WHITEY: My name is Sparky.

BRONSKI: That is Sparky.

EMILY: Not with his brain in that condition.

BODINE: And you know what condition. You can't expect someone's brain to be okay if they've just fallen out of a roller coaster.

BRONSKI: It happened several years ago.

WHITEY: I fell out of a roller coaster and so what? I don't even know my own name.

MANITAS: Who's that?

EMILY: It's the people who have been sent for to fix him up.

BRONSKI: Give up.

WHITEY: Not give up.

BRONSKI: He's witless.

SPARKY: And stop that laughing.

WHITEY: What is your name and what can you do?

BODINE: Antonia. Let me put my hands on his head. It will help me tell.(*She rises and stands behind WHITEY.*)

SPARKY: Tell what?

BODINE: Tell what is wrong and then I can cure him. *(She puts her hands on WHITEY's head.)*

EMILY: Go ahead.

BODINE: Alright, I can tell.

SPARKY: You can't tell anything. Don't believe her. It's only a trick. Tricksters!

BRONSKI: Goathead !

BODINE: Silence, a moment of silence.

LEE: You are very tired and sleepy.

WHITEY: Don't try and hypnotize me.

SPARKY: Tricksters, hucksters!

MANITAS: Shut up.

WHITEY: Heads will roll.

MIRANDA: Are you sure you remember? First you...

BODINE: Don't tell me. I know what I'm doing. Would you like a book?

WHITEY: Yes.

SPARKY: Don't touch it. It's the book of the dead.

SMITH: Exactly.

BODINE: Osiris awakes. The wary god wakens, the god stands up. Stand up, thou shalt not end, thou shalt not perish. The world is losing its grip. A moment of silence, a moment of silence. What's your name?

WHITEY: You remember my name.

BODINE: What is your name, Sparky?

WHITEY: I told you it doesn't work.

LEE: A moment of silence.

BODINE: A moment of silence.

LEE: A dark period.

MIRANDA: A moment of silence.

WHITEY: Though I walk through the valley of shadows I feel no evil.

BODINE: It's just a shadow.

LEE: Pay no attention to the man behind the curtain.

SMITH: Whitey.

WHITEY: Sparky.

BODINE: Are you seen from way below? Are you?

WHITEY: Believe me, I am. I was crumpled out of it.

BODINE: And then?

WHITEY: I don't know why I am so uncomfortable here.

BODINE: And then?

SPARKY:*(Stands)* It's worse than the movies or the Catholic church. All tricks done with mirrors and strings . And the bullfights, the bullfights! Everyone knows that bull gets up again. They just dust it off and send it back into the ring for the next fight. Everyone knows that! *(Sits)*

WHITEY: Bagpipes.

LEE: Off with his head .

BODINE: You are rampant, delirious, dehydrated, bald of all thought and action.

SMITH: Say it again.

BODINE: You are rampant, delirious, dehydrated, bald of all thought .

WHITEY: And I will always be with you until you run out.

BODINE: Sing it again, say it again.

LEE: Remove all doubt.

WHITEY: Wait a minute.

BODINE: No. *(Sits)*

MIRANDA: Remove the doubt.

WHITEY: Wait a minute.

BODINE: No.

MIRANDA: Remove the doubt.

WHITEY: I will always be with you until my bulb burns out. I am an act of love.

SMITH: Remove the doubt.

SPARKY: It's all tricks.

BODINE: The shred, once upon a time there was a shred.

WHITEY: Get me out of here. Get me out of here, I said.

BODINE: Numbness, getting numb. One of you is totally deluded. Angrily so. Oh, so angrily so.

WHITEY: It's yelling at itself.

SMITH: The poor exhausted flies, the maggots died of hunger, the deer flesh was all eaten up, they broke their teeth on the bones, the tried but they died of hunger and fantasia.

WHITEY: That would be nice and then the light came into the room and destroyed everything.

BODINE: Blew it away. Tell me what you are seeing.

WHITEY: I'm seeing light come into the room and blow everything away. One of you is accused of murder and the other...you have the right to remain silent.

SPARKY: I will.

BODINE: Order in the court, monkey wants to speak.

WHITEY: I don't want to set the world on fire. Got a match?

EMILY: He's delirious. Whitey.

LEE: Delerioso.

EMILY: Whitey.

WHITEY: Tell it to the judge.

SPARKY: This is ridiculous. I won't have it.

MANITAS: You will have it.

SPARKY: One is stupid, one doesn't know what to think.

WHITEY: But you're wrong. I do want to set the world on fire. I want to burn it all down to shreds. *(Laughs)*

EMILY: Whitey!

SPARKY: Whitey!

WHITEY: Sparky!

BODINE: A spark is a shred of light.

WHITEY: You have to do it or you won't win.

BODINE: Do you want to win?

WHITEY: I want to win.

MIRANDA: Do you want to win over god and the devil?

BODINE: And the deep blue sea?

WHITEY: Yes, I do.

BODINE: Do you ever have a burning desire to fail and burn with god in heaven?

WHITEY: Yes, yes, yes.

SPARKY: This isn't funny , he's retarded.

MANITAS: I wish you'd be a little nicer to them after all they've done.

SPARKY: Oh, alright. Sorry.

MIRANDA: You see, we all have to adapt to each other.

BODINE: I want to make it clear and precise.

LEE: Lights, shadows, reflection, translucence, do you understand?

BODINE: The Milky Way is in your face.

LEE: That's right, dear.

MIRANDA: That's right, dear.

SMITH: Try and get a little rest.

WHITEY: I don't want a little rest.

BODINE: That's right dear, try and get some rest.

WHITEY: I don't want some rest. Where are my pants?

CUT

(Stage is dark.)

SCREENS: (Window image and table switch screens. The table image is closer now and viewed from a lower angle. The size of the window image remains the same. WHITEY, SMITH, MIRANDA and LEE sit around the table. BODINE stands.)

MIRANDA: How do you feel?
WHITEY: What do you care?
LEE: We really do. We want to help you.
WHITEY: Help me what? Why don't to help them.(Motioning off screen.)
BODINE: They don't need any help right now.
SMITH: When the time comes.
WHITEY: And when will the time come?
MIRANDA: Why do you ask so many questions?
LEE: Let him ask, that's good.
WHITEY: Why is it good?
BODINE: Because it is good.
LEE: If you ask questions you get answers.
WHITEY: I'm not getting any answers.
SMITH: Yes, you are.
MIRANDA: Every time we ask you something you get an answer.
BODINE: Do you see?
WHITEY: Yes, I see.
LEE: He understands.
WHITEY: No, I don't see or understand.

MIRANDA: Yes, you do.
WHITEY: I don't.
LEE: You do.
WHITEY: I do. I'll understand anything you want me to .
BODINE: It's difficult.
WHITEY: When will I be able to see?
LEE: Close your eyes.

(WHITEY closes his eyes.)

MIRANDA: What do you see?
WHITEY: Blue.
BODINE: There, you're beginning to see.
WHITEY: I am.
SMITH: Do you see me?
WHITEY: I don't know.
SMITH: What do I look like?
WHITEY: You are tall and you have red hair.
SMITH: Yes. And what does Miranda look like?
WHITEY: Short with blue hair.
MIRANDA: Right.
BODINE: You can see.
SMITH: How many windows does this room have?
WHITEY: Five on one side and six on the other.
LEE: Correct.
SMITH: How many fingers am I holding up?

(His hands remain down.)

WHITEY: Six on one and five on the other.
SMITH: Right.
LEE: And what is your name?
WHITEY: My name is Whitey.
LEE: Right.
BODINE: And what do you look like?
WHITEY: I am tall with black hair.
SMITH: Right.
MIRANDA: You see?
BODINE: Now you can go.
WHITEY: I'll go. How did you do it?
LEE: Just by suggesting.
BODINE: And you believed us and so you can see.
SMITH: Come back some time.
BODINE: Come back some time. Do you hear me?
WHITEY: Yes.
MIRANDA: Come back some time.
BODINE: Alright?
WHITEY: How did you do it?
LEE: You did it.
SMITH: Come back some time.
WHITEY: I'll be back.
LEE: Do you understand?
WHITEY: Yes, I understand the problem.
LEE: The problem is to bring rationality to bear in an inherently irrational situation.
SMITH: Exactly.

MIRANDA: You seem tired.

WHITEY: I am.

BODINE: What was that dream you had?

WHITEY: Oh, there was this strange orange frog lizard iguana with red orange eyes and green whites. It was trying to stare the other smaller lizards down, trying to convince them but they wouldn't pay attention to him so the dream ended.

LEE: That was some kind of a bad snooze.

WHITEY: If you have to kill for breakfast then you shouldn't get up.

BODINE: Try not to think about it.

SMITH: Try not to think about it.

WHITEY: I want to think about it.

MIRANDA: But don't. You'll confuse yourself.

SMITH: Come over here to this window.

(WHITEY follows SMITH as he walks off frame and into the frame of the screen opposite. They stand on either side of a window and look out.)

LEE: Look out it.

BODINE: Do you see out?

MIRANDA: What do you see?

BODINE: Tell me what you see.

WHITEY: Water, trees, wind.

LEE: Is it nice?

WHITEY: Yes.

MIRANDA: Think about what you see.

(Table and window images switch screens.)

BODINE: And don't think about anything else.
SMITH: When you go back, have a rest.
WHITEY: Are you trying to trick me?
BODINE: No, not at all.

(Table and window images switch screens)

WHITEY: Alright.
LEE: What is the sky like?
WHITEY: Pearly iridescent.
BODINE: It's okay, you're alright, the ace of spades is dead.
WHITEY: Is that true?

(Table and window images switch screens)

SMITH: The answer is absolutely yes.
BODINE: When you came here, you were seventy pounds, voiceless, sightless, mindless, heartless, incriminated, a drop of water in a cracked glass.
WHITEY: Nothing, I fell out of a roller coaster.

(Images of table and window switch screens)

MIRANDA: That's all?
SMITH: That's all.
WHITEY: That's true.
BODINE: And now?
LEE: And now the high altar was made low,
the low sky was made high, and the blue sky
was made red and god was satisfied.
BODINE: And now it's clear, he's fixed in
hindsight.
SMITH: And now you can return.
MIRANDA: Do you want to go back?

(Images of table and window switch screens)

WHITEY: Yes. Thank you.
SMITH: Come and visit.
WHITEY: Thanks for helping me.
BODNE: You're welcome.
SMITH: Thank you.
MIRANDA: What's my name?
WHITEY: You are Miranda, and you are
Smith, and you are Lee
and you are Bodine.
MIRANDA: Right.
WHITEY: Thank you.
BODINE: Come and visit any time.
WHITEY: And I am Whitey.
MIRANDA: Whitey.
LEE: Yes.
WHITEY: I'm fixed.

CUT

(WHITEY is now seated onstage at the mirror topped table. SPARKY, BRONSKI, MANITAS and EMILY are each sitting at one of the tables. They occasionally eat from the plates in front of them.)

SCREEN A: *The four figures of SMITH, BODINE, MIRANDA and LEE are seated at a blue table. The table is seen from a slightly lower angle than the last scene. Each figure eats from an empty plate. BODINE smokes.*

SCREEN B: *The large window seen previously. Both screens will alternate image several times during the scene.*

SPARKY: ...because of that and so thank you for repairing his eyes.
BODINE: You're welcome. If there's anything else we can do.
BRONSKI: Bodine, how did you discover the treatment?
BODINE: Oh, it wasn't me.
SMITH: It was Lee. She's been working on it for years.
BODINE: I couldn't have done it without my colleagues.
LEE: And collaborators.

MIRANDA: And such a gentle way to approach things.

SMITH: We believe that is the best way.

MIRANDA: A more sensual approach to the senses.

BODINE: How old is the boy?

WHITEY: Nine years old.

MIRANDA: How old are you?

SPARKY: Nine years old.

BRONSKI: But it was his eyes.

LEE: Oh, yes it was his eyes. He was totally sightless.

BODINE: It's as if they had been melted away out it some kind of shock.

SPARKY: We were doing a test on the roller coaster. He was sitting in the front and flew out.

EMILY: He told us.

BRONSKI: You look a little pale, Whitey.

SMITH: You think so?

MIRANDA: He'll be all right.

LEE: He'll be all right.

BODINE: When will the park be operational?

SPARKY: Not for several months.

BRONSKI: The accident was widely publicized even though we tried to keep it quiet.

EMILY: Whitey was our best technician. He conceived the entire course. He decided to ride it alone that day.

BODINE: More broccoli?

WHITEY: Of course.

MIRANDA: And Sparky, what do you do?

SPARKY: I work on the spark plugs, the spark elements...I do a lot of soldering.

LEE: And Manitas?

MANITAS: I build a lot of the engines.

LEE: Of course. I can tell. Your hands, such beautiful hands.

MANITAS: Thank you.

SMITH: Is most of it computerized?

EMILY: A lot of it is computerized.

SPARKY: Except for the sparks.

MIRANDA: Emily, what do you do?

EMILY: I handle the business end and sometimes I play records during the rides.

LEE: And I'm sorry, I've forgotten your name.

BODINE: Bronski.

BRONSKI: I'm not involved. I'm just a friend, and advisor.

MIRANDA: Chew that well, Sparky.

SPARKY: I'm chewing, I'm chewing....

EMILY: The needle on the turntable is screwy.

SPARKY: I know. I'll fix it.

(He rises and begins roaming about the space lip syncing a deep voiced man's recitation of a fragment of Pablo Neruda's poem "Te Recuerdo Como Eras" (I Remember You As You Were). He punctuates various phrases by gracefully gesturing towards the actors on stage and screens with his hands.)

"Eras la boina gris y el corazón en calma.
En tus ojos peleaban las llamas del crepúsculo.
Y las hojas caían en el agua de tu alma.

Apegada a mis brazos como una enredadera,
las hojas recoían tu voz lenta y en calma.
Hoguera de estupor en que mi sed ardía.
Dulce jacinto azul torcido sobre mi alma.

Siento viajar tus ojos y es distante el otoño:
boina gris, voz de páajaro y corazón de casa
hacia donde emigraban mis profundos anhelos
y caían mis besos alegres como brasas.

Cielo desde un navio. Campo desde los cerros.
Tu recuerdo es de luz, de humo, de estanque en
calma!"

LEE: Where did you learn that?
SPARKY: I made it up.
BODINE: It's quite beautiful.
SMITH: You must come and recite it.
SPARKY: Oh, no thanks.
MIRANDA: Oh, you must.
SPARKY: I'll be busy in the shop. (*He fiddles with the needle on the record player and sits back down.*) The needle's fixed.
EMILY: And what do you do?
MIRANDA: I don't do anything but I don't have to.

SMITH: *(Motioning towards the window.)*
Did we show you?
BRONSKI: No.
LEE: Look.
BODINE: It's quite beautiful, isn't it?
MANITAS: Yes, it is.
WHITEY: How far to the other side?
SMITH: About twenty miles.
MIRANDA: In the winter it's covered with ice.
BODINE: In the summer it's broiling.(Lights cigarette.)
LEE: What color is it?
WHITEY: Blue.
MANITAS: It's so blue.
SPARKY: Why is it so blue?
BODINE: It's the translucence of the air, the moisture in the air. Even our breath makes it blue. The thousands and millions of panting birds in the atmosphere combine with it all. All the smoke from anything that ever burned anywhere. And the wind blows it all around and mixes it up and then the vibration from every sound that's ever made heats it with the sunlight.
SMITH: And makes it blue.
EMILY: But why does it end up blue and not red?
LEE: Because all these things harmonize to make it blue.

MIRANDA: And if they don't then the sky will get to be red or purple or green.
LEE: But mostly red.
MANITAS: Have you ever seen it red?
SMITH: Once or twice.
LEE: Even the rain was red.
MIRANDA: I hate it when it's red.
BODINE: But it's almost always blue. Always blue, one blue or the other.
But it almost always stays blue.
SMITH: Always blue.
BODINE: Blue always.
LEE: Except when something goes wrong.
SMITH: But that's very seldom.
MIRANDA: And thank god for that.
BODINE: But if something goes off and it goes red, the blue usually swallows it up.
LEE: And it's purple around the edges for a few minutes or days.
SMITH: When will the park become operational?
WHITEY: In one or two months if we work hard.
MANITAS: And do you have many patients?
SMITH: Oh, a lot.
LEE: We see them day to day.
BRONSKI: Do they all get fixed?
BODINE: Oh, almost all.
EMILY: And the ones that don't?
LEE: They go away.

MIRANDA: It's very sad when there's nothing to be done.

BODINE: What color do you see?

WHITEY: Blue.

MIRANDA: It's very sad but there's nothing to be done.

SMITH: Where is Pinry?

EMILY: Over there.

BODINE: Hello, Pinry.

SMITH: Why do you talk to that puppet?

WHITEY: It's a doll puppet.

BODINE: But why do you talk to it?

SPARKY: Sometimes it talks back.

BRONSKI: And it's quite wonderful.

SMITH: I see.

LEE: Will it talk tonight?

SPARKY: Probably not.

EMILY: It's very shy. *(Picks up puppet and pets it. She passes it to the others.)*

MIRANDA: Did it always talk?

BRONSKI: Not always but one day it just spoke.

LEE: And what did it say?

BRONSKI: It said "ojo caliente."

WHITEY: It means hot eye in Spanish.

MIRANDA: Ojo caliente.

LEE: That suggests red.

EMILY: Oh, no.

SPARKY: It suggests a very strong iron blue.

BODINE: Will it talk tonight?

EMILY: I don't think so. It only talks to us but it hears everything.

It always hears everything and stores it up in its brain. He's quite friendly when he gets the chance.

MANITAS: But he gets sad sometimes.

WHITEY: We put him in front of the window and he gets better.

SMITH: Maybe we can help him.

BRONSKI: Oh no, he doesn't need any help.

LEE: Are you sure?

SPARKY: We're sure.

MIRANDA: Are you sure, Pinry?

WHITEY: He says he's sure. He's okay.

LEE: Where did he come from?

SPARKY: We found him in the street.

EMILY: He didn't talk for months and then he said it. "Ojo caliente."

BODINE: But what does that mean?

WHITEY: Hot eye, the eye that sees it all.

BRONSKI: It sees every thing, every way.

SMITH: But where did he come from?

LEE: How can he be alive?

BRONSKI: He just is.

BODINE: Maybe he was a dead man once and he was inhaled into the doll and made it alive.

EMILY: I don't think so.

BRONSKI: The doll has always been alive. Right, Pinry?

MANITAS: That's right.

BRONSKI: So he'll stay here with us.
MIRANDA: Can he come and visit us sometime?
MANITAS: I don't think so. He likes it here.
SMITH: But maybe he'd like it here.
EMILY: We'll ask him and he'll tell us eventually.
LEE: But he looks like he'd like to stay here.
BODINE: He's quite nice.
MIRANDA: Is his head wooden?
WHITEY: Oh, yes.
LEE: Does he dance?
SPARKY: Oh, sometimes at night when I play records. *(He hands the puppet to Emily.)*
EMILY: He can jump very high.
BRONSKI: But no strings.
BODINE: Oh, no strings?
SMITH: Who does he belong to?
BRONSKI: He doesn't belong to anyone.
SPARKY: I found him on the street one day.
EMILY: And it was Whitey's birthday.
WHITEY: And I went home one day and I opened that present and it was the puppet. But he doesn't really belong to anyone.
SPARKY: He likes to sing.
MIRANDA: What does he sing?
WHITEY: All kinds of songs.
EMILY: A lot of blues.
MANITAS: Crazy blues.
MIRANDA: He must come and visit.

EMILY: We'll ask but I think he'll say no. *(She puts the puppet on Manitas' table.)*
BODINE: Does he like electronic music or wooden music?
BRONSKI: Both. Because he is wood. But he loves electric too.
SMITH: I see.
MIRANDA: I wish he would sing now.
MANITAS: Pinry, do you want to sing?
WHITEY: I don't think so.
EMILY: Maybe if we play he'll sing.

(Stage performers gather around MANITAS' table.)

LEE: Let's try it.
SPARKY: We'll sing and you play.
BODINE: We'll get our instruments.
SMITH: What shall we play?
SPARKY: Oh, anything.

SCREEN A: cuts to BODINE, SMITH, MIRANDA and LEE playing instruments: French horn, violin, piano and banjo.)

(Live actors lip sync "All in the Game" by the Four Tops.)

STAGE ACTORS: Many a tear has to fall,
BRONSKI: But it's all in the game.
STAGE ACTORS: All in the wonderful game...

MANITAS: …that we know as love.

WHITEY: You had words with him…

SPARKY: …and your future's looking kind of dim.

EMILY: But these things your heart will rise above.

WHITEY: Whoah, whoah,whoah…

STAGE ACTORS: Once in a while he won't call…

SPARKY: Mmhmm…(Music stops, screen actors stop playing.)

WHITEY: Picking up puppet and hugs it.) Did you sing?

EMILY: I don't think so.

MANITAS: No, he didn't.

MIRANDA: And what do you advise them on?

BRONSKI: Oh, on lots of things. This and that.

LEE: What kind of things?

BODINE: How long have you known the puppet?

BRONSKI: I've known the puppet longer than they have.

SPARKY: You didn't tell us that?

BRONSKI: Yes I did.

SMITH: How long have you known him?

BRONSKI: A few years. Five or ten.

WHITEY: You never told us that.

BRONSKI: He belonged to some friends of mine but he was so insulting that they threw him out. So I picked it up out of the garbage.

Then I came home one night and he'd disappeared. Then these guys found him on the street.

EMILY: You never told us that.

BRONSKI: It never occurred to me that it was the same puppet till right now.

He's changed a lot. His face used to be quite sour. He's not insulting anymore.

He used to be a strange hideous little puppet child but he's changed.

MIRANDA: The poor thing.

LEE: Well, what do you have to say for yourself?

BODINE: Say something.

WHITEY: You are not to be trusted.

EMILY: How could you deceive us?

SMITH: Leave him alone. I'm sure he's had a hard time.

WHITEY: Pinry, how could you deceive us?

EMILY: He's just a puppet for god's sake.

BRONSKI: What do you have to say for yourself?

MIRANDA: He's not talking.

EMILY: I don't think he will for a long time now.

SPARKY: We've upset him and now he's upset.

MANITAS: How can you tell?

SPARKY: His face has absolutely no expression.

EMILY: Absolutely expressionless.

BRONSKI: Mindless.

WHITEY: He's thinking in there somewhere in that wooden head.

SPARKY: It's no big deal really.

EMILY: Maybe if we play catch with him he'll speak.

SPARKY: Don't.

EMILY: He loves it.

(The stage actors toss the puppet from one to the other. It finally lands in Emily's arms.)

LEE: Any expression?

EMILY: No.

SPARKY: Not a thing.

MIRANDA: The poor thing.

LEE: Let us see him.

MANITAS: I think he wants to stay down here.

BODINE: Let him think for himself.

SMITH: Pinry, do you want to stay there?

WHITEY: No answer.

SPARKY: Let's just leave him.

WHITEY: Put him to sleep.

EMILY: Let him have some nice puppet dreams.

BODINE: Goodnight, Pinry.

SPARKY: You little wooden pygmy.

MANITAS: Sweet dreams, my dear little woodenhead.

CUT

(MANITAS, BRONSKI, and SPARKY are asleep at their tables. EMILY and WHITEY begin to investigate the projector boxes.)

MIRANDA appears on SCREEN A and LEE on SCREEN B. Each is seated at a blue topped table, viewed head on, eye-level, medium close up. MIRANDA and LEE will alternate screens several times during the scene.)

LEE: **Don't touch that.**
WHITEY: Why?
MIRANDA: **Sipping a glass of wine.) Don't touch that, I said.**
EMILY: What is it?
LEE: **Just don't touch it.**
WHITEY: But what is it?
MIRANDA: **It's a machine.**
EMILY: What does it do?
LEE: **Nothing much.**
MIRANDA: **It makes a light.**
WHITEY: Why?
LEE: **No reason in particular.**
EMILY: But why? *(EMILY and WHITEY wave their fingers in front of the projector beams and make shadows.)*
MIRANDA: **It's a lamp. It's not to be touched.**
LEE: **It could hurt you.**
WHITEY: What's it connected to?

LEE: Nothing.

MIRANDA: Don't get too near it.

LEE: Don't do that.

EMILY: What?

MIRANDA: Don't do that. Don't put your hands there.

LEE: You're making shadows.

MIRANDA: Don't do that. Don't ever do that.

WHITEY: It's fun.

LEE: Please stop.

MIRANDA: Do you want us to lose our patience?

EMILY: We're curious.

LEE: Curiosity killed that cat.

WHITEY: Is that what killed it?

MIRANDA: Yes, the cat made to much of a shadow.

EMILY: How can you be such an authority on this?

LEE: We've been around.

WHITEY: How can you continue to believe in that theory?

MIRANDA: Don't touch that.

LEE: It may cause a massive problem for which we may have to create a massive solution.

MIRANDA: Have some wine.

WHITEY: No, thank you.

LEE: Oh, please do.

EMILY: Why are you always offering us wine?

MIRANDA: I love wine.

EMILY: Why?

MIRANDA: **It's a wonderful drink, it's wonderful. It's sensual and as you know, I'm a sensualist.**

WH1TEY: I didn't know that.

LEE: **Have some.**

EMILY: No thanks.

MIRANDA: **And what is your problem?**

WHITEY: Nothin', I didn't say nothin'.

LEE: **Where do you live?**

EMILY: I live right here.

WHITEY: I think you'd better stop drinking that.

EMILY: You're starting to get tipsy.

MIRANDA: **I know.**

WHITEY: Well, you're going to tip over.

MIRANDA: **So what if I do?** *(Drunk.)*

LEE: **So what if she does?**

MIRANDA: **Where's the puppet?**

EMILY: He's around.

WHITEY: What do you want with that puppet?

LEE: **We just like it.**

EMILY: Everyone likes it.

LEE: **Does it really talk?**

WHITEY: Sure.

MIRANDA: **When can we see it talk?**

EMILY: You're getting too drunk now.

MIRANDA: **I am not.**

WHITEY: Why do you always stay up there? Why don't you come down here?

MIRANDA: We don't want to.

EMILY: Why not? You keep asking us to go up there and you never come down here.

LEE: Up is better than down.

EMILY: Why is that?

MIRANDA: Just is.

LEE: I just wish that kid would do his poem again. He's so good at it.

EMILY: Sparky, wake up and do the poem.

SPARKY: What for?

WHITEY: Just do it. She wants you to.

SPARKY: *(Lip syncs poem while half asleep in his chair.)*

Eres la boina gris y el corazon en calma.

En tus ojos peleaban la llamas del crepusculo y las hojas caian del agua de tu alma.

Apegada a mis brazos como una enredadera, las hojas recogian tu voz lenta y en calma.

(Falls asleep.)

LEE: That's wonderful. *(Falls asleep.)*

EMILY: Why don't you come down here?

MIRANDA: I told you.

WHITEY: Hey, she fell asleep.

MIRANDA: She always does.

EMILY: So come down here.

MIRANDA: Oh no, I can't.

WHITEY: Come on, why not?

MIRANDA: I can't, I'm a coward.

EMILY: What's to be scared of?

MIRANDA: A lot. I'm sorry, I can't because if I do you see, I won't be able to come back and . . . *(Falls asleep.)*
WHITEY: She's lost consciousness.
EMILY: They both have.
WHITEY: Hello!
EMILY: Hello!
WHITEY: Bodine!
EMILY: Miranda!
WHITEY: What the hell were their names again? *(Touching the projector box.)*
LEE: Don't touch that.
EMILY: I thought you were asleep.
LEE: We never sleep.

CUT

(BODINE and SMITH on Screen A. MIRANDA and LEE on Screen B.)

LEE: We want the puppet.
EMILY: What for?
MIRANDA: Because we do. We want to talk to it.
SMITH: We're losing our patience.
WHITEY: Patience for what?
BRONSKI: We are losing our patience.
MANITAS: Well, you can have it.
SMITH: What's the matter with you?
SPARKY: Nothing at all.

BODINE: Whitey, come here.

LEE: Tell them we want the puppet.

WHITEY: Why do you want the puppet?

SMITH: Maybe we can help it talk.

SPARKY: It's fine the way it is.

BRONSKI: So leave it.

EMILY: Where is it?

MIRANDA: Something wrong?

MANITAS: No.

MIRANDA: You're going through withdrawal.

SMITH: Screensick. You're being unpoisoned, that's all.

WHITEY: There's nothing wrong with me.

BODINE: What color do you see?

LEE: Screensick.

SPARKY: Blue.

LEE: Something wrong?

MANITAS: Is that like seasick or homesick?

WHITEY: Or maybe you can shut up.

BODINE: Whitey.

LEE: See what you have become. What's happened to you?

MANITAS: Maybe you can just shut up for a minute and let me think.

SMITH: Alright.

BODINE; Emily, why don't you leave the room?

EMILY: I will not leave this room.

LEE: Give me your undivided attention.

EMILY: No thanks.

SMITH: Look at my face.

EMILY: No thanks, I don't like your face.

BRONSKI: Excuse me, do we have any privacy?

LEE: We don't need any of your advice.

MANITAS: Leave us alone, will you?

BODINE: You're becoming deluded. We've helped you and now you are...

MIRANDA: So ungrateful. You act like we're not even here.

SMITH: You're turning a deaf eye to us.

LEE: What color do you see?

BODINE: What color do you see?

WHITEY: Would you please leave?

BRONSKI: I'm starting to see red.

MANITAS: You're wrapped around their fingers.

MIRANDA: You're seasick. You're tired.

EMILY: You're being intercepted.

BRONSKI: Anticipated.

EMILY: Don't you see that?

MANITAS: Would you please leave?

LEE: What for?

MANITAS: We'll have to disrupt you then.

BODINE: And how will you do that?

SMITH: We'll wrap you around our fingers.

MANITAS: We'll cut them off.

WHITEY: I will disrupt you.

MANITAS: I can figure it out. There's a way.

LEE: I doubt it.

MANITAS: I will disrupt you. Interrupt you.

SMITH: Momentarily perhaps.

MIRANDA: Look at this blue. Feast your eyes on it.

EMILY: Don't look at it.

BODINE: That's O.K., you will be correctible, erasable.

BRONSKI: And so will you.

LEE: We are indelible.

BODINE: You will be correctible.

WHITEY: I will be incorrigible.

SMITH: We will remedy that.

WHITEY: So okay, fine.

SPARKY: Incorrigible.

SMITH: The world is so small, we must all be civil to each other.

SPARKY: Get out of here.

MIRANDA: You will finally come to understand the way things are done.

EMILY: But I have come to understand.

LEE: Relax.

WHITEY: I don't want to relax.

MIRANDA: But you've got to.

BODINE: We'll leave now.

SMITH: We'll be back.

BRONSKI: Please don't come back for awhile.

MANITAS: Wait 'til the sky is more blue than it is.

BRONSKI: As you can see, it's become quite red.

SMITH: I like red sometimes.

BRONSKI: I don't.

SMITH: Things can't always be all blue.

SPARKY: That's not what you said before.

LEE: Things can't always be all blue.

WHITEY: That's not what you said before.

BODINE: We changed our minds.

LEE: It's okay when things get red.

WHITEY: The hell it is.

SMITH: It is.

MIRANDA: Shall we play a song?

LEE: Of course, that will ease things.

BODINE: Things can become bluer then.

LEE: The blues then.

SMITH: The blues.

WHITEY: I don't want to.

MIRANDA: Come on.

BRONSKI: Don't do what they say.

MANITAS: Come on, we'll calm them down.

EMILY: They're always calm.

BRONSKI: They're trying to trick us.

BODINE: We are not.

SPARKY: You're trying to convince us into something.

LEE: Try not to think about it.

SMITH: Come on, let's play.

SPARKY: I think they should leave,

BODINE: Come on.

SPARKY: My hands hurt.

SMITH: Of course they do, you little junkie.

SPARKY: What?

CUT

(Stage players lip sync "Master of Eyes" by Aretha Franklin. EMILY sings lead, the others sing backup.)

(Screen A: BODINE, LEE, SMITH and MIRANDA accompany them on instruments.

Screen B: Window.)

EMILY: *"One look in your eyes, baby just turns me on.*
So inviting to me, you know I feel that they're my own.
And I, I had to surrender my sense of pride. Your touch from behind on my shoulder, on my shoulder so tender. The deepness of your eyes. I can't stop lovin' you baby…The deepness of your eyes. I can't stop lovin' you …"

(Music and lights cut abruptly.) **(Both screens go dark.)**

EMILY: Of course you can't you little junkie!
SPARKY: Of course I'm a little junkie,so what I can work like that, it helps me, I can pay for it, I make enough. *(Picks up puppet.)*
WHITEY: And you don't spend money on anything else.

MANITAS: What else is there to spend money on? Vitamins? Movies?

SPARKY: It helps me to be graceful.

BRONSKI: Graceful.

EMILY: You're ruining your angel face.

WHITEY: And you're ruining your angel face. You're in love with that scavenger, that vulture.

BRONSKI: The others are vultures. She is not.

MANITAS: They're all vultures and they'll have us all up there if they get their way.

BRONSKI: And that will be the end of the Milky Way.

SPARKY: They'll suck us out of our space. They'll rot our space up. How can you let them do that? Don't you see what they're doing?

BRONSKI: You're a deluded little junkie.

SPARKY: Even the puppet can see what's happening.

WHITEY: They're convincing you, they're tricking you but they won't get me.

BRONSKI: How can you talk that way about them after all they've done for you? SPARKY: They're watching us, listening to us.

MANITAS: They can't hear us.

EMILY: God forbid if they do.

WHITEY: You're so ungrateful.

SPARKY: Just shut up.

BRONSKI: Don't tell him to shut up.

EMILY: He can say what he wants.

BRONSKI. And turn us against them after they fixed Whitey?

SPARKY: Whitey fixed himself. Manitas, you're so silly, you'll be the first to go.

WHITEY. There's nothing wrong with them. I've been up there and come back. Nothing happened. It's no big deal. We should send you up there.

SPARKY: What could they do to me?

BRONSKI: Un-junk you.

SPARKY: Nothing could convince me to go up there.

WHITEY: And stop playing with that doll.

SPARKY: It's my friend. It's our friend. It's not like them, right Pinry? Hush little baby, don't you cry. *(Hugs puppet.)*

EMILY: Stop it you lunatic.

BRONSKI. When are they coming again?

MANITAS: Whenever they want.

EMILY: What's that noise?

SPARKY: There's no noise.

(Screen A: Blank. Screen B: MIRANDA walks into a dingy room through a dark doorway and walks forward until half her body fills the screen. She is holding a glass of wine from which she occasionally takes a sip. She is seen from slightly below eye level.)

MIRANDA: *(Smiling.)* **Hello! Is anyone there?**

MANITAS: Of course we're here.

MIRANDA: Can I come in?

BRONSKI: Of course.

MIRANDA: Manitas, I want to know if you could come and fix my car engine, we don't know what's wrong with it. Maybe you could tell us, advise us.

SPARKY: Don't go.

MIRANDA: What?

MANITAS: Sure, no problem.

BRONSKI: Don't go.

MIRANDA: Maybe you'd all like to come.

EMILY: No thanks, we're busy.

WHITEY: I'm not.

SPARKY: Whitey, don't.

WHITEY: What's the big deal?

SPARKY: If you go, be careful.

WHITEY: What do you mean Sparky?

SPARKY: Nothing.

BRONSKI: Too many needles. Don't listen to him.

MIRANDA: Maybe Bronski would like to come. I'm sure Bodine would like to see you.

BRONSKI: I'm sure she would.

MANITAS: Cut it out.

SPARKY: The smell of veins exploding.

MIRANDA: Have some candy.

(Screen: Slow zoom to extreme close up of Miranda's face.)

EMILY: *(Rises and walks to the screen with Miranda on it.)* No thank you, I don't eat sugar. But did I ever tell you about when I was a little girl in Montana I used to ride the six o'clock train that left with the coffins in the morning. I'd sit and do my homework on top of the coffins. It was me and the train master alone with the dead people in the coffins. When the coffins would be moved off the train, my cousin would meet us. She'd throw her voice because she was a ventriloquist. She'd have the coffin say "Let me down easy, boys."

MIRANDA: What a stupid story.

EMILY: I think it's fascinating.

MIRANDA: I don't.

EMILY: And so I accepted death at a very early age.

MIRANDA: Your sentiments are ugly.

EMILY: Thank you.

MIRANDA: What is this change of heart?

WHITEY: Don't mind them.

BRONSKI: Spark plug blew.

SPARKY: I'm inside a chestnut. Rotten from the inside out.

MIRANDA: You are.

MANITAS: Oh please, don't be so negativistic.

SPARKY: Go fix that car, will ya?

MIRANDA: Listen little boy, morning will come and you'll still be dead and the day will

go on into the night and the year will keep going and that's how I ended up.

SPARKY: Oh, no I won't because . . .(*Gets up and walks away from his table.*)

WHITEY: Where are you going?

SPARKY: (*He begins reciting "Heroin" by Lou Reed. He wanders languidly around the entire playing space in large circles. The others sit watching and smoking.*)

"I don't know just where I'm going but I'm gonna try for the kingdom if I can because it makes me feel like I'm a man. When I put a spike into my vein and I tell you..." etc...and I guess I just don't know, oh and I guess I just don't know." See how the needle goes down so gently and softly?

(*He gently places needle on a revolving record.*)

(*Miranda in close up switches screens.*)

MANITAS: Stop talking about that record player.

WHITEY: I'll break those turntables

SPARKY: Don't make me live without them.

WHITEY: You'll live without them.

SPARKY: Oh, no I won't.

WHITEY: Oh, yes you will.

SPARKY: Oh no I won't. Just shut up.

BRONSKI: Don't tell him to shut up.

EMILY: He can say what he wants. I'll break those turntables.

MIRANDA: Well now they've changed their story.

EMILY: From what to what?

BRONSKI: First they say that if we go up there, we can come back. Then Manitas wants to go up there and we know she won't want to come back *(Sparky picks up puppet)*

MIRANDA: I never said that

MANITAS: They said that we wouldn't have to stay up there.

EMILY: And we don't.

SPARKY; It's your only way out.

MIRANDA: Your future's looking dim.

BRONSKI: Why?

MIRANDA: It just is from here, from what I can see.

SPARKY: Why?

MIRANDA: You're almost in tears.

MANITAS: I don't like this game.

MIRANDA: You have to play it.

BRONSKI: But I don't want to, you play it.

SPARKY: I already did and I'm out.

EMILY: You can't be out.

MIRANDA: That's because he's stupid.

BRONSKI: Don't blame him because he's stupid.

MIRANDA: It's his own fault that he's stupid.

WHITEY: It is not.

SPARKY: They're standing in there waiting with sharp knives.

MIRANDA: You seem to be in a mild state of hysteria.

SPARKY: I am. *(Throws puppet to floor.)*

CUT (Screens go blank.)

EMILY: I get these headaches.

BRONSKI: From thinking.

MANITAS: Think harder.

BRONSK1: I'm trying.

MANITAS: If we agree to go up there.

BRONSKI: If we do, we'll all be stuck.

MANITAS: Well, we all don't have to go.

EMILY: Just one first.

WHITEY: Then another.

BRONSKI: One by one and take them over.

EMILY: Won't work.

MANITAS: I'm going to try to do something. Let me go up there first.

EMILY: They'll keep you up there.

MANITAS: Who cares? We can't stay trapped in here like this.

WHITEY: Don't do it.

MANITAS: Watch something. Watch this. See what happens when I do this? *(Puts hands in front of projector lens.)*

EMILY: It makes a shadow.

BRONSKI: To us it does.

MANITAS: But to them? Didn't you notice that when we did that they told us to stop? It bothers them somehow.

EMILY: If we do everything they tell us not to.

WHITEY: Then what? MANITAS: Then maybe we can break something down.

BRONSKI: And the projectors?

EMILY: If we touch them.

BRONSKI: Break them, knock them over.

WHITEY: That won't work.

EMILY: How do we do it?

MANITAS: Pull the plug.

EMILY: No don't, not yet. Pinry's stuck up there.

CUT

(*SPARKY runs behind screen into a large storeroom and begins climbing a ladder as if searching for something.*)

EMILY: I can feel them resonating, radiating everywhere around us. They can see us, they can hear us, everything.

WHITEY: They can not. They left the room.

BRONSKI: Just because they left the room it doesn't mean they're not here.

WHITEY: Where do they go when they go away?

MANITAS: Into the wires, just like electricity.

EMILY: How shall we do this?

BRONSKI: We have to anticipate them.

MANITAS: Intercept them.

BRONSKI: But now they come and go whenever they want.

SPARKY: Pinry's gone.

EMILY: Where?

SPARKY: He's gone, they took him.

MANITAS: How do we know that?

SPARKY: He's not here.

WHITEY: Maybe he went out.

EMILY: He never goes out.

MANITAS: Then, where is he?

SPARKY: I don't know. I've looked all over. He's nowhere.

WHITEY: He has to be here somewhere.

SPARKY: He isn't. I looked everywhere.

BRONSKI: What did you do with him?

SPARKY: Nothing. He was listening to a record and I fell asleep and he was gone.

WHITEY: Pinry.

BRONSKI: Pinry.

MANITAS: They've got him.

SPARKY: Then we have to get him.

WHITEY: What do we need him for. He's just a puppet.

EMILY: How do we go up there?

WHITEY: The same way I came off, through a wire.

MANITAS: I just agree to go up there the next time they ask.

BRONSKI: Here comes someone.

(Screen A: BODINE, medium close-up, blue background. Screen B: SMITH, medium close up in front of a blue background, sobbing. Screens switch every few lines. These faces will from now on be seen from progressively lower angles. When they speak to stage players, their focus is downward.)

SMITH: Hello.

EMILY: Good morning.

SMITH: I'd like to talk to you.

BRONSKI: Fine. Come in. Where's the puppet? Where's Pinry?

SMITH: The puppet is dead. He hung himself.

SPARKY: Impossible.

SMITH: Possible, Probable. A fact. The fact is that he is dead.

BRONSKI: The probability or the possibility is that one of you hung him up.

SMITH: Why would we do that?

EMILY: I'm sure you have your reasons.

SMITH: That's impossible.

BRONSKI: You can't kill a puppet.

SMITH: But you did.

EMILY: Shut up. You're trying to confuse me.

SMITH: The fact is that someone killed him and someone has to pay.

MANITAS: Get off it.

SMITH: My advice is to . . .

EMILY: We don't want your advice.

SMITH: You need my advice.

SPARKY: Where is Pinry?

SMITH: Hung up somewhere, wherever one of you hung him.

SPARKY: You're confusing us, deliberately confusing us.

SMITH: But how can we be? We have always been very clear.

SPARKY: Deliberately confusing us.

SMITH: I am trying to clarify.

MANITAS: What? Is something wrong?

BODINE: I want to make something very clear.

SMITH: I want you to understand something.

MANITAS: *(A pause of few seconds.)* Well, what is it?

BODINE: Do you realize that . . . ? I've got to figure out a way to tell you this, to make it make sense to you. I want to explain it to you so that it makes sense to you. I know it will sound ridiculous. Do you see the machines? They're the projectors. They are projecting you.

EMILY: You must be kidding.

BRONSKI: You are the ones that are being projected.

BODINE: You're silly.

MANITAS: We are here. You're up there.

EMILY: You are the projection.

BRONSKI: Once upon a time someone put you on emulsion and projected you. You're all wound up on the film and I can prove it to you . . .

MANITAS: By turning off the projector.

BODINE: Because you'll turn yourselves off and then what?

SMITH: Stop and think. You'll shut yourselves off and then what?

BRONSKI: I'll show you.

BODINE: You're headed for the brink.

MANITAS: Idiotic.

BRONSKI: Sooner or later the film will run out and we'll see who ends up on a roll. EMILY: And it won't be us.

BODINE: It will be you. WHITEY: This is impossible.

SMITH: You'll see.

BODINE: What we're trying to make you realize is that you must get off that roll of film so that when the film runs out you'll be safe.

WHITEY: We are safe.

BODINE: But believe me.

WHITEY: It's not true.

BRONSKI: I'll turn off the projector and then we'll see.

SMITH: You have to realize that you're chained into that machine and if you don't get out of it, you'll be stuck in there forever. Can you understand that?

BODINE: Is that clear?

SMITH: Don't you feel yourselves slipping away?

BODINE: You're just shadow and light and sound.

SMITH: Pieces of things.

EMILY: No.

BODINE: Believe us.

EMILY: Can't believe that.

SMITH: I hope you understand that we are running out of time and that we'll have to try every way we can to help you. You may not understand but you'll thank us in the end.

WHITEY: Thanks, but no thanks.

BRONSKI: What are they talking about?

WHITEY: I don't know really. I don't remember.

MANITAS: You're really nice but I don't think you know what you're talking about.

(Screen: An extreme close up of WHITEY's eye replacing BODINE for fifteen seconds.)

BODINE: If there was only some way we could convince you before it's too late.

MANITAS: Listen, you people are nut brains.

SMITH: Think, think hard. Somewhere deep down in your thought machines it must make sense to you.

SPARKY: It doesn't make any sense.

BODINE: It's unchangeable. We're trying to help you figure it out.

SMITH: Why are you letting yourselves run out?

EMILY: I don't want to figure it out.

MANITAS: Thanks for your concern but as you can see we're just not concerned. How can you ask us to believe something so illogical.

BODINE: We're not asking you. We're telling you.

SMITH: You're so unwise. Think, think harder.

WHITEY: I don't like thinking so hard.

SMITH: Think about it. Figure it out. It makes sense.

EMILY: There's nothing to figure out.

SMITH: You'll die in the darkness.

BODINE: You're so unwise.

SMITH: What are we telling you, some kind of story?

BODINE: Do you think we're lying to you?

WHITEY: No.

BRONSKI: I guess. It's got to be some kind of story.

EMILY: It's got to be some kind of story.

SMITH: I'll tell you a story.

BODINE: Where is your sympathy for yourselves?

(Screens A &. B: During the following story, an extreme close up of WHITEY's eye appears on both screens simultaneously for fifteen seconds. It cuts to BODINE and SMITH.)

BRONSKI: But let me tell you the story. One day we lived on the bottom of the world. We'd like to tell you a story about how we live. You might be surprised. At my father's funeral the dogs cried and vomited. We were so sad and one fine day the swans on the lake died. There was such a weird sound early in the morning he died. The dog chewed the chain 'til all his teeth fell out. The shepherd had not gone far when he heard a tiny voice. The mouse and the ant lived happily ... la ormigita y el raton, And the bread was moving in there all by itself.
EMILY: What a stupid, stupid story.
SMITH: Now that is a story. It's a story that's not particularly true and these are the facts. Those are the machines and you are coming out of the machines.
EMILY: No more stories.
WHITEY: Prove it then.
MANITAS: How can we prove it? There's no way to prove it, except by turning off the projectors and we know you won't do that.
SMITH: Go ahead and see what happens.
BODINE: There's no way to prove it except by turning off the projectors and you know we won't do that.
EMILY: Scare us.

BRONSKI: Let's see what happens.

BODINE: Or what un-happens.

WHITEY: They picked my brain apart and put me back together again. Convinced me.

EMILY: I know it without a doubt.

BRONSKI: I appreciate you're trying to be our guiding light but I don't believe you.

SMITH: Without a doubt.

BODINE: I know it without a doubt. And you know what certain words mean.

EMILY: One at a time.

(BODINE and SMITH speak simultaneously.)

SMITH/BODINE: Without a doubt. You have a beginning and an end and now you must find the middle.

WHITEY: Okay, no more stories. I don't believe them. Now, one at a time.

BODINE: No one asked you to believe.

EMILY: You might be but I'm not.

MANITAS: Either we are or we aren't.

SPARKY: We aren't.

CUT

(Screens A & B: Faces of LEE, SMITH,BODINE,MIRANDA in close up alternate rapidly according to who is speaking.)

LEE: I want to make it clearer again.

BRONSKI: I don't want to hear anymore.

MANITAS: Bite the dust, will you?

MIRANDA: I hate dust.

EMILY: Okay, so you hate dust, now get lost.

SMITH: Listen to me.

EMILY: I don't want to listen to you.

SPARKY: You're all weird.

LEE: You are going to end up in a can.

MANITAS: You are going to end up in a can.

BODINE: Your lamb is in a puddle. You're a brahma bull in Chicago. Don't you understand what I'm trying to tell you?

SPARKY: Cut the hoi polloi.

BRONSKI: The houi-houi.

MANITAS: Fade away.

LEE: Not fade away.

MIRANDA: We're losing our patience.

EMILY: I've heard that.

BODINE: We're trying to bring rationality to bear in an inherently irrational situation.

BRONSKI: I've heard that before too.

(BODINE's voice falls out of sync.)

BODINE: Just beware that when the rules of your irrational, illogical behavior become in excess, our policy will be one of swift and effective retribution. In other words we're going to pull the plug.

EMILY: Pull it.

BODINE: But we live in an area of limits to our powers.

LEE: Let it also be understood that there are limits to our patience. You're becoming rabid, bleeding, flagrant.

WHITEY: No more stories.

BRONSKI: I know what you mean chili bean.

EMILY: It's over, it's finished. It's not important.

SPARKY: You're trying to convince us. To trick us.

SMITH: What color do you see?

(BODINE's voice returns to synch.)

BODINE: You're digging your own grave with your own . . .

LEE: Sprockets.

SMITH: I'm not leaving 'til you listen to me.

BODINE: The world is so small we must learn to be civil to one another.

EMILY: Get us out of here.

SMITH: You're going through withdrawal.

SPARKY: You people make me sick. (*Spits food.*)

LEE: We're trying to intercept you.

BODINE: Anticipate, contracept, intercept.

BRONSKI. You're an idiot, a ticket taker, a shadow, an administrator, a slam dancer, a projectionist, a dramaturg, so get lost.

BODINE: I am all those things and I can inhale you and burn you up. We can inhale the smoke and make fuel out of you. We can make fuel out of anything. Does that shock you?

EMILY: Yes, it shocks me,

SMITH: It should and when you're through with your inky little plot to pull the plug, I will disrupt you.

EMILY: Momentarily perhaps.

BODINE: You will be correctible.

LEE: Erasable.

MIRANDA: Incorrigible.

SMITH: Simpleton, use your mind.

LEE: You will finally come to understand.

BODINE: That you are our own projection, our own creation, our postcard if you will.

EMILY: I won't.

BODINE: Yes you will and it has been recorded.

BRONSKI: The hell we are.

LEE: We?

EMILY: You.

MIRANDA: You forget that you're about as brainless as that puppet.

SPARKY: I hate the way you smell.

BODINE: Your angel face is only a shadow.

MIRANDA: Do we smell?

EMILY: Stop trying to edit me you bureaucrat, social climber, user, flatterer, crystal blue persuader, pigfucker, pancake. *(Throws bread roll at screen.)*

LEE: You're out of control.

BRONSKI: What did you say?

BODINE: Pancake.

SMITH: And so we administrate.

EMILY: Flapjack.

- 71 -

BODINE: You should be thankful. It is our pleasure, our inspiration, our duty, our dedication, our configuration. You are arrogant, ungrateful.

LEE: I'm sorry, there's nothing more we can do for you. I'm sorry, I really am.

EMILY I'm horrified.

BRONSKI I thought you said you were sorry

BODINE: I never said that.

BRONSKI: I know what you mean chili bean I know exactly what you mean.

SMITH: Help comes from above, trouble from below.

MANITAS: The sun comes through the window. I can help myself.

SPARKY: What color do you see?

SMITH: No color. Look at your friend, you know what happened to her.

MANITAS: I don't know nothin'.

SMITH: You don't know nothin'.

LEE: Bury the hatchet.

BODINE: Why is he shaking?

SMITH: He's afraid.

MANITAS: Get lost.

BODINE: I will. For a while.

(*Screens go dark.*)

BRONSKI: Why are you shaking?

SPARKY: I'm afraid. I'm not brave, I never was.

EMILY: You're out of control. Relax.

SPARKY: I can't, I'm only nine years old. I get these headaches.

MANITAS: Well, stop getting them.

SPARKY: I'm going to keep getting them because I'm out of junk. *(Runs to MANITAS.)* Can I ask a dumb question?

EMILY: What?

SPARKY: Is the Milky Way still in my face.

MANITAS: Yes

SPARKY: No it isn't. You know it isn't, tell me the truth.

EMILY: All right, it isn't.

SPARKY: I get these headaches and shaking. They told me if I go up there I'll stop.

BRONSKI: Hold on a little while.

SPARKY: I can't, I'm only nine years old. They can help if I go up there.

WHITEY. They say they can.

SPARKY: They can. I know they can.

EMILY: They can't.

SPARKY: Well then, who is going to help me?

EMILY: I don't know.

MANITAS: We're out of food too.

SPARKY: Then we have to go up there.

BRONSKI: Hell no, I'm not going up there with those putrid face, puke mouths.

SPARKY: Well I'm going to eventually. I can just tell. I can't hold on any longer.

EMILY: I'm going to give them the puppet.

BRONSKI: They have the puppet.

EMILY: They have a fake puppet and they know it and they know we know it.

BRONSKI: And we know they know we know they know it.

EMILY: And the puppet knows it.

BRONSKI: And the puppet is very sad.

MANITAS: Then give them the puppet.

EMILY: I will. I want to see what's going on up there.

SPARKY: There's nothing going on up there. It's just shadows and light,

BRONSKI: Haven't you seen enough?

EMILY: I have and I don't want to see anymore, I'm giving them the puppet and if I don't get out then I don't get out. Look at me when I talk to you. Everything has been educated against itself, every proportion in this room is conspired against itself. Everything is contradicted. I'm finally convinced that I want to see what it is because I can't understand this anymore.

MANITAS: You are so graceful, so silent. Don't make your face angry. It is so ugly.

EMILY: It is ugly. It will be ugly.

BRONSKI: Please don't show me that face.

EMILY: I will show you that face. I will show you that face. I will always show you that face forever. It is ugly, it will be ugly because of them.

BRONSKI: Don't show me that ugly face, don't make it ugly and angry.

EMILY: It will be ugly and angry and mad and terrible and brutal. Brutal brutality. You'll get no love from my face ever again. You'll never see me again. The film will run out and you'll never see me again, so remember my ugly, brutal and angry face that they have created. This is no angel face no more, sweet and innocent and graceful no more. It has another meaning now.

SPARKY: Where is your diginity?

EMILY: I have no dignity. I can spit on you from up there. No more, Sparky, no more, No more Milky Way. This is the end of the Milky Way. Welcome to the end of the film. Welcome to the end,

BRONSKI: This is an act of hate.

EMILY: It's an act of love.

BRONSKI: Where is your dignity?

EMILY: That's my dignity up there.

SPARKY: What does that word mean?

EMILY: It doesn't mean anything. It's an act of dignity and hate. The two are tied together. Stop the projector, don't make me do this.

BRONSKI: I'm not. Don't make me do this. Don't make me.

EMILY: The poor exhausted flies, the maggots died of hunger, the deer flesh was all eaten up, they broke their teeth on the bones, they tried but they died of hunger and fantasia.

MANITAS: Where will you go?

EMILY: Somewhere out into outer space. Hopelessly out into outer space, alone. Want this coat?

SPARKY: Sure. (*EMILY throws her coat to SPARKY.*)

(*The stage goes dark. Sparky, wearing Emily's coat, stands alone at center table.*)

(Close-up of BRONSKI's face on Screen A. Screen B: Close-up of burning candle.)

BRONSKI: Sparky.

SPARKY: What? Where are you?

BRONSKI: Over here.

SPARKY: Where is Manitas?

MANITAS: Here. It's me. I'm a candle now.

SPARKY: Why?

BRONSKI: She thought she had the jump on it but she didn't and now she's a candle.

MANITAS: Wax.

SPARKY: What is it?

BRONSKI: They were right.

SPARKY: What do you mean they were right?

BRONSKI: You've got to get up here quick.

SPARKY: Why?

BRONSKl: They were right.

SPARKY: How could they be right? Manitas told me that they were wrong and that we should stay here.

BRONSKI: You can't stay there. You'll run out and that'll be it. They were trying to save us. Get Whitey and get up here before it runs out. It's running out. Save yourselves.

SPARKY: I don't believe you.

BRONSKl: Believe me, I'm telling the truth.

SPARKY: You are not. You're lying.

BRONSKl: Look at Manitas. She didn't believe them and now she's a candle.

SPARKY: How could they turn her into a candle?

BRONSKl: It was the light. She screwed up. Believe me, save yourselves. Wake up Whitey.

SPARKY: I don't believe you.

BRONSKI: Don't pull the plug.

SPARKY: I'm going to pull the plug on you. I don't believe you.

BRONSKI: You've got to.

SPARKY: I can't.

BRONSKI: Please, you're shaking, you're out of junk. I can tell. They can help you up here if you come right now they can fix you up.

SPARKY: It's not true.

BRONSKl: It has to be true.

SPARKY: They changed you.

BRONSKl: No one changed me.

SPARKY: You're a coward and they changed you. You're not brave, you never were. You're not loyal, you never were.

BRONSKI: I am loyal. That's why I'm trying to help you. Believe me.

SPARKY: I can't believe you. I can't believe you. I know you can't help yourself.

BRONSKl: I can help myself and I can help the two of you.

SPARKY: You can't help us because you're stuck up there. If you can help us then come down here and help us pull that plug.

BRONSKl: If you pull the plug you'll kill yourselves.

SPARKY: So then we will.

BRONSKl: Don't do it.

SPARKY: We have to. I'm not going to be convinced or persuaded.

BRONSKl: Can't you see what's going on?

SPARKY: I can see what's going on. I believe my own eyes.

BRONSKl: Think, think.

SPARKY: I don't want to think anymore.

BRONSKl: Touch your skin.

SPARKY: No.

BRONSKl: Touch your skin.

SPARKY: You touch my skin, then we'll know what's what.

BRONSKl: You know what.

SPARKY: I'm sorry, I don't believe you.

BRONSKl: Alright, be clever and don't believe me but you'll be sorry.

SPARKY: You're trying to trick me.

BRONSKI: I'm not. Please believe me. I'm your friend. If you don't believe me I don't know what else I can do if...
(Screens go blank.)
SPARKY: Bronski, come back!

CUT

(SPARKY is visible through Screen A standing behind a large tilted white tabletop. Whitey is alone on stage at center table)

(Screen B   EMILY, extreme close-up of face. Screen A   Emily's eyes, extreme close up.)

EMILY: Whitey, Sparky.
SPARKY Where are you?
EMILY: Over here.
SPARKY What happened?
EMILY: Listen to me.
WHITEY: Can they hear?
EMILY: I think so.
SPARKY: What shall we do?
EMILY: Hide yourselves.
WHITEY: Where?
EMILY: Anywhere.
SPARKY What's going on?
EMILY: Don't let them find you.
WHITEY: They've found us anyway. They'll find us again.
EMILY: They'll see whatever we do.

SPARKY I've got to get some stuff. I can't, I'm hungry, I'm starving.

EMILY: Don't let them see you.

WHITEY: What shall we do?

SPARKY: Don't believe her.

WHITEY: Why?

SPARKY: They're all lying up there.

EMILY: Believe me.

WHITEY: Shall we smash the projector?

EMILY: No, don't.

SPARKY: What do we do?

EMILY: If you can somehow make everything black

WHITEY: What for?

EMILY: Black everything out.

SPARKY: How?

EMILY: Paint it so they can't see you and turn the projector backwards. Rewind it.

SPARKY: It won't go.

EMILY: Yes it will. If you can rewind it back to the beginning.

WHITEY: Impossible.

EMILY: It works. They were talking about it, I heard them.

SPARKY: We can't rewind it. There's no button.

EMILY: Yes there is. Somewhere.

WHITEY: We checked and checked and checked.

EMILY: Keep looking. There is a button. There's a way to do it.

SPARKY: How do you know?

WHITEY: Do you believe her?

EMILY: Listen to me. Watch this. Watch what I did. I got a knife and I went in there and look.

(Screens A & B: Jumbled pieces of film, the faces of BRONSKI,MANITAS,SMITH etc. rush by, jump cuts. Screen A returns to EMILY, Screen B is blank.)

SPARKY: Bronski!

EMILY: Did you see what I did?

WHITEY: How did you do it?

EMILY: The razor's edge. But that's no remedy, you've got to turn it back. Backwards until the beginning, that's the only way.

SPARKY: We'll think about it.

EMILY: Don't think too long. If they find out and see what you're doing. You have turn it back and cut them up.

WHITEY: But we don't know how.

EMILY. You can just cut them out of it.

SPARKY: I don't believe you.

WHITEY: You're trying to make us wreck it all.

SPARKY: I can't stay here much longer. I'm cold, I'm freezing.

EMILY: Turn it back.

SPARKY. No don't. Don't believe him.

WHITEY: What about Bronski and Manitas?

EMILY: Do you believe them? Everyone has their own configuration about this and now you've got to think and figure it out. But don't just sit there. If you can somehow make it all black first, then they can't see you. Believe me, it's the only way to do it. There is only one way.

WHITEY: There's no way.

SPARKY: I'm cold. (Lays on table.)

EMILY: There's only one way to do it. There is only one way because I heard them saying that . . .

CUT *(Screens go black momentarily. Screen A: MANITAS, medium close up seen from above, sitting at blue table Screen B- Close up of burning candle.)*

(SPARKY, asleep on a table behind Screen A, is visible through MANITAS's image.)

MANITAS: Whitey.

WHITEY: Yes, where are you?

MANITAS Up here, up here. Where's Sparky?

WHITEY: He's asleep. He's been up all night trying to find a way out of the projector. What's going on up there? Where is everyone?

MANITAS: Asleep.

WHITEY: Can they hear you?

MANITAS: Probably, I'm sorry.

WHITEY: What is it? Where are you now?

MANITAS: I'm just a vagabond, floating around in the emulsion now.

WHITEY: I was right. Where is everyone else?

MANITAS: They're here too but we hardly see each other.

WHITEY: Why?

MANITAS: We just don't. It depends what pieces of film we're on. Sometimes yes, sometimes no.

WHITEY: What can we do?

(MANITAS switches to Screen B, candle to Screen A.)

MANITAS: Pull the plug.

WHITEY: No, if we pull the plug, then you'll all be gone.

MANITAS: Turn the projector backward.

WHITEY: It doesn't go backwards, no rewind.

MANITAS: It's going to run out. Stay where you are.

WHITEY: You're trying to trick me. You're like them now. You're trying to trick me, convince me.

MANITAS: I'm not. Trust me.

WHITEY: I can't.

MANITAS: It's going to run out and us with it. You should be glad.

WHITEY: I don't believe you.

MANITAS: Believe me.

WHITEY: I don't know.

MANITAS: You know, you have a brain, think, touch your own skin. Feel it?

WHITEY: Yes.

MANITAS: It's going to run out and us with it. Where's the doll?

WHITEY: The doll? It's dead I think. Sparky's shaking, he can't go on much longer.

MANITAS: He has to.

WHITEY: I don't believe you. They've changed you.

MANITAS: They haven't. Think.

WHITEY: I can't think any more.

MANITAS: Let it run out.

WHITEY: We'll see, we'll see.

MANITAS: We'll see. I'm going now. I can see myself coming up on the projector again. (Screen A: Close up of MANITAS's eyes upside down, moving across screen.)

WHITEY: Touch me.

MANITAS: I can't.

WHITEY: Are you going to be on again?

(SPARKY leaves table behind screen and walks onstage.)

MANITAS: I don't know, I can't tell. I'm not brave, I never was.

WHITEY: Get me out of here.

MANITAS: No, stay there.

WHITEY: I don't believe you. I don't believe you.
MANITAS: **Believe me because if you can just . . .**

CUT

(Screens go dark.)

(As WHITEY stares at the empty screens SPARKY surprises him from behind and pushes him violently into a chair)

SPARKY: Alright. Tell me everything you know.
WHITEY: I don't know much. All I know is this story.
SPARKY: Then forget the story, forget it. Cut out the lights and forget the story. Have you forgotten it?
WHITEY: Yes.
SPARKY: Tell me what you remember.
WHITEY: The dogs chewing the chains and that's it.
SPARKY: That's it?
WHITEY: That's all.
SPARKY: Now forget that. Have you forgotten it?
WHITEY: Yes.
SPARKY: Tell me what you remember.
WHITEY: The chewing.

SPARKY: Alright, now forget that.
WHITEY: Alright.
SPARKY: Now what do you remember?
WHITEY: Nothing, nothing at all.
SPARKY: Tell me what you know.
WHITEY: Nothing.
SPARKY: What is your name?
WHITEY: Nothing.
SPARKY: What is your name?
WHITEY: Nothing.
SPARKY: Fine, now we can start again.
WHITEY: With nothing.
SPARKY: (Puts his hands on Whitey's head.)
We will resurrect you from nothingness. From
nothing. Your name is Whitey. Yes.
WHITEY: And the chewing dogs.
SPARKY: I thought you said you forgot that.
WHITEY: I did.
SPARKY: Don't lie. Forget it, forget the
chewing dogs.
WHITEY: I have.
SPARKY: What is your name, Whitey? Your
memory is in the minority, the inferiority.
WHITEY: Exactly.
SPARKY: You will have no references to
anything but what is happening right now and
you can speak again.
WHITEY: And my name is Whitey.
SPARKY: Put your ear to the ground and
listen. (Pushes Whitey's head onto table.) How
do you feel?

WHITEY: Mesmerized. My name is Whitey. I smell a rotting banana.

SPARKY: What is a banana?

WHITEY: A banana is a book.

SPARKY: Right. You smell a rotting book.

WHITEY: I'm sad about something but I don't know what it is. Something's walking around up there.

SPARKY: And you don't know what it is. You are inside out.

WHITEY: Inside out.

SPARKY: And don't look back. Don't look back. Remember the pillar of salt, the pillar of salt. Would you like a book or something? Touch me, do you feel my skin? (Turns his back and holds his hand behind him.)

WHITEY: Yes. (Touches Sparky's hand with his index finger.)

SPARKY: Don't break the rhythm. Don't look back. Touch my skin.

SPARKY: Why?

WHITEY: Why?

SPARKY: Why are you trained to a razor's edge?

WHITEY. You've put yourselves back

(Screens A & B: Extreme close ups of BODINE, LEE, MIRANDA, SMITH alternate with lines.)

BODINE: We are losing our patience.

SMITH: You can't escape our influence.

LEE: We're trained to a razor's edge.
SMITH. Why?
MIRANDA: Because we have to be.
SMITH: We can teach you to depend on us.
LEE: On our honest good will.
BODINE: We can teach you to pretend and how to deal with this mess
you've created for yourselves out of yourselves.
SMITH: We can teach you to tear every moment apart bit by bit, softly and
put it back together again properly, the way we have been.
WHITEY: You've put yourselves back together again?
SPARKY: To a razor's edge?
BODINE: Yes.

CUT

(Both screens blank.)

WHITEY: It's all broken. (Throws chair across the stage.)
SPARKY: We'll fix it.

(Sparky appears behind Screen B behind large rectangular white tabletop.)

WHITEY: I can't believe that.
SPARKY: You'd better believe it.

WHITEY: I'll never believe anything again.

SPARKY: So fake it.

WHITEY: Wait 'til Sunday.

SPARKY: It is Sunday.

WHITEY: I don't care. Stop playing that piano.

SPARKY: No.

WHITEY: Stop it. I'll smash it up.

SPARKY: And then I'll smash you up. Your nose will be a bloody red tomato.

WHITEY: Get that piano out of your brain.

SPARKY: What are we going to do?

WHITEY: Where's that stupid doll puppet?

SPARKY: What for?

WHITEY: Maybe it knows something.

(Picks up puppet from floor.)

SPARKY: That wooden head don't know a thing. Leave it alone, it's sad.

WHITEY: Upset?

SPARKY: It can't think anymore than we can.

WHITEY: *(To puppet.)*Say something. Tell us what to do, How can we get them back? …..Really?

SPARKY: What's it saying?

WHITEY: It's not saying anything.
(Throws it violently into chair,}

SPARKY: You must sit and think. Think, think.

WHITEY: I can't think.

SPARKY: Think. WHITEY. I can't, can't.

SPARKY: Think about it, think about it.

WHITEY: Think about it yourself.

SPARKY: My brain can't.

WHITEY: Your brain.

SPARKY: My brain can't. It can't go anymore. It's stopped up.

WHITEY: Think about it.

SPARKY: I don't want to think about it.

WHITEY: My brain is corroded. It won't go anymore.

SPARKY: What are we going to do?

WHITEY: It's a hopeless case.

SPARKY: What does that word mean?

WHITEY: I don't know what it means god damn it.

SPARKY: Then, goddamn you.

WHITEY: We can't figure our way out of this.

SPARKY: We're done for.

WHITEY: Done for what, birdbrain?

SPARKY: You're a birdbrain.

WHITEY: An innocent birdbrain.

SPARKY: You're a poor polluted, corrupted little brain.

WHITEY: My brain's out of control, it won't work.

SPARKY: De-organize it.

WHITEY: I can't, it's organized and wrecked.

SPARKY: Then throw your brain out and use your hands. One by one they turned us around.

WHITEY: They had to testify.

SPARKY: They betrayed us.

WHITEY: My friends will never betray me.

SPARKY: Yes they will, the way you did.

WHITEY: I did not. That wasn't me up there. I don't know who that was.

SPARKY: Why don't you give in. Admit they already did.

WHITEY: They did not.

SPARKY: They don't care about you. If they did, they wouldn't have left you high and dry.

WHITEY: They won't ever do that.

SPARKY: They will because they already did.

Why don't you admit it now everything has to change.

WHITEY: No, I'm going to hold out.

SPARKY: You're crazy. High and dry.

WHITEY: What a way to go.

SPARKY: I'm going.

WHITEY: Then go. You're a coward.

SPARKY: I'm not brave, I never was. I'm going. I'm sorry. Goodbye.

WHITEY: See you around.

SPARKY: Maybe we'll end up in the same can.

WHITEY: I doubt it. SPARKY: Please let me go.

WHITEY: Alright go. Get lost.

CUT

(Screen A: wide shot of long rectangular room. SPARKY at far end, face bloody. Screen B: identical empty room.)

SPARKY: Whitey.

WHITEY: Sparky get out of there.

SPARKY: I can't.

WHITEY: Why did you go up there?

SPARKY: I had to. I was hungry and cold and I got to get fixed up. I've got to get fixed up. Whitey, help me.

WHITEY: How? Why did you do it? Where is everyone?

SPARKY: I don't know. I don't see anyone. Get me off of here. Touch my skin, wake me up.

WHITEY: Do you hear anything?

SPARKY: No. It's all blue everywhere. How do I get out of here. Get me out of here. I'm bleeding get me out of here. (Runs back and forth between walls.)

WHITEY: Where are they?

SPARKY: Whitey. Whitey.

WHITEY: Who is it?

SPARKY: It's me, Sparky.

WHITEY: Where are they?

SPARKY: They went out.

WHITEY: Don't talk too loud. They might hear you. What shall we do?

(SPARKY runs off Screen A and appears on Screen B.)

SPARKY: I know what to do. I heard them talking.

WHITEY: About what?

SPARKY: Remember when they said something about tearing every moment apart bit by bit?

WHITEY: The razor's edge.

SPARKY: Right, well that's it.

WHITEY: About how they put themselves back together again?

SPARKY: Right. Well if they put themselves back together again, then you can take them apart.

WHITEY: How?

Sparky runs from Screen B and appears on Screen A.

SPARKY: In the machine, the projector.

WHITEY: How?

SPARKY: Stop the projector.

WHITEY: I can't. I checked. There's no button, no plug.

SPARKY: Then break it.

WHITEY: If I break it, won't be able to fix it.

SPARKY: So what? Then they'll be gone.

(Screens A & B: SPARKY runs back and forth between walls.)

WHITEY: And you will too.

SPARKY: I don't care.

WHITEY: You'll all be smashed up inside the machine.

SPARKY: Then that's the way it'll have to be,

WHITEY: Do you want to get out of there?

SPARKY: Yes.

WHITEY: Then come down.

SPARKY: I can't.

WHITEY: Why can't you?

SPARKY: I can't. I don't know how. (Feels wall.)

WHITEY; Yes you do.

SPARKY: I don't know how, I can't.

SPARKY: Show me how. I can't.

WHITEY: You can.

WHITEY: I can't show you. You have to know how. You have to know how.

SPARKY: I can't, I can't. There's no way out, there's no way off.

WHITEY: Try.

SPARKY: I have tried.

WHITEY: And what happens?

SPARKY: There's a brick wall.

WHITEY: There's no brick wall here. I don't see one.

SPARKY: Yes   there   is. (Kicks wall)

WHITEY: Do you want to get out?

SPARKY: Yes.

WHITEY: Well, why did you go up there?

SPARKY: I just wanted to see what it was like and now I can't get out

WHITEY: Do you want to get back?

SPARKY: Yes I do. I want to, I want to, I want to.

WHITEY: Do you want to?

SPARKY: Stop asking me that I want to, I really want to but I can't. There's no way. I don't know how.

WHITEY: Please.

SPARKY: How? How do I do it? There's no way.

WHITEY: Isn't there a crack or something in the wall?

SPARKY: Yes, but it's very small. It's too small to get through.

WHITEY: Try. Push.

SPARKY: It's too small. (SPARKY runs frantically between walls, opposite screen shows identical image upside down)

WHITEY: Try again.

SPARKY: I keep trying and I can't. It's just a tiny crack. There's no way.

WHITEY: Goddamn you.

SPARKY: Oh, goddamn you. It was your idea for us to go up there and now I can't get back and it was your idea and now the crack is too small and I can't get back and you keep asking me and now what can I do? I really want to get off and I

can't. There's just no way, just ain't no way.

WHITEY: You know how to do it and you're just not doing it. You're just like them and you won't do it. You want me to stay up there, you want to, you want to.

SPARKY: I don't want to. Help me.

WHITEY: I can't help you. I don't know how.

SPARKY: Yes you do. You can tell me something to help me. You must know something.

WHITEY: You help me.

SPARKY: I can't do it. I can't do it. Get me out of here.

WHITEY: Why did you do it? Why did you go up there?

SPARKY: I don't know why I did. You wanted to go up here.

WHITEY: I did but I never thought you couldn't get back.

SPARKY: You tricked us into getting here and now we can't get back.

WHITEY: I never tricked you.

SPARKY: And now they're going to come back and take me away.

WHITEY: Not if you get away first.

SPARKY: But I can't, I can't.

WHITEY: Kick the wall.

SPARKY: I keep kicking and kicking until my feet are bloody and I can't anymore. I can't anymore, I can't, I can't. I can't.

WHITEY: Do you want to get out of there?

SPARKY: Help me.

WHITEY: I can't help you.

(SPARKY falls into the corner of room. Zoom from wide shot of room to medium close up. Opposite screen shows identical image upside down.)

SPARKY: Goddamn you. Help me get out of here. They're coming back.
WHITEY: Kick. Push.
SPARKY: I can't. They're coming, I have to go and hide.
WHITEY: Hide where?
SPARKY: I don't know, they can see me, they'll find me in here.
WHITEY: Kick.
SPARKY: I can't, they're coming.
WHITEY: I don't know how to help you.
SPARKY: Do something.
WHITEY: I can't do anything.
SPARKY: You can't do anything?
WHITEY: I can't.
SPARKY: Help me, they're coming.
WHITEY: Show me.
SPARKY: There's no way. Whitey,Whitey.
WHITEY: Where are you?
SPARKY: Whitey, where are you?
WHITEY: Turn on the lights.
SPARKY: Whitey!
WHITEY: Where are you?
SPARKY: Whitey, it's me, Sparky. It's me. Say something. No don't, don't say anything,

don't say anything. Hide. Don't let them find you.

(Whitey hides under mirrored table.)

(SPARKY, now extreme close up, remains on Screen A)
BODINE, MIRANDA, LEE, and SMITH appear on Screen B, extreme close up.)

BODINE: Whitey.
SMITH: Answer us. Come on.
MIRANDA: We know you're there.
SPARKY: He's gone. He's not here. He left.
SMITH: He can't leave. There's no way out of this.
SPARKY: He left.
LEE: Shut up Sparky.
SPARKY: No.
SMITH: Shut up.
BODINE: Whitey, don't. Don't be a child.
SMITH: Say something.
MIRANDA: Sooner or later you'll have to.
LEE: (*Sings*) "I don't want to set the world on fire." Whitey, what are
you doing?
SMITH: You are so graceful, so silent. Don't make your face angry. It is so ugly. SPARKY: It is ugly. It will be ugly.
WHITEY: Please don't show me that face.

(Screen B: SPARKY in corner upside down, medium shot.)

SPARKY: I will show you the face. I will show you that face. I will always show you that face forever. It is ugly, it will be ugly because of you.

MIRANDA: Don't show me that ugly face, don't make it ugly and angry.

SPARKY: It will be ugly and angry and mad and terrible and brutal. Brutal brutality. You'll get no love from my face ever again. You'll never see me again. The film will run out and you'll never see me again, so remember my ugly, brutal and angry face that they have created. This is no angel face no more, sweet and innocent and graceful no more. It has another meaning now. You've made me a mess.

MIRANDA: Where is your dignity?

SMITH: No more Sparky, no more.

SPARKY: No more Milky Way. This is the end of the Milky Way. Welcome to the end of the film. Welcome to the end, monster.

SMITH: This is an act of hate.

SPARKY: It's an act of love.

LEE: Where is your dignity?

(Screen B: Large window.)

SMITH: What does that word mean?

SPARKY: It doesn't mean anything. It's an act of dignity and hate. The two are tied together. Stop the projector.

WHITEY: Don't make me do this.

SPARKY: I'm not.

WHITEY: Don't make me do this. Don't make me.

SPARKY: We'll just live without them.

(*Pause.*)

WHITEY: Where will you go? (Gets out from under table.)

SPARKY: Somewhere out into outer space. Hopelessly out into outer space. Alone. Alone. I will be dreamy and sad, dreamy and sad, always dreamy and sad for a very long-time and I will last forever because I am on film and it will be my pleasure to play you over and over and over again for my pleasure and freedom and my inspiration. I will play you over and over and over again until you are shredded year after year, year after year for a thousand years, real soft and real loud whenever I want, however I can, whenever I want because after that that's all I'll be able to do, over and over again for a thousand years because that's all I'll ever know how to do by then and I'll just keep doing it and I'll just keep playing over and over again for you, over and over again until I turn to shreds and when I turn to shreds you'll still hear me in your brain cavity over and over again for a thousand years and you'll always feel free because of that and even when they say I don't have a brain I will have a brain because I will have a brain because I do have a brain because I am a brain because the brain is right there in the plug or in your hand or in the light bulb or in the emulsion or the groove or whatever, in the plastic for a thousand years even without electricity or whatever, over and over again because I do have a brain and I can sing if I want to because I can sing, because I can. Is that right? Do you understand me? Right? What is your name?

WHITEY: Whitey.

SPARKY: You'll always remember my name.

WHITEY: What did you say?

SPARKY: Nothing.

WHITEY: That's what I thought.

SPARKY: What is your name?

WHITEY: Whitey.

SPARKY: Whitey.

WHITEY: You'll remember my name.

SPARKY: Always, always and forever, forever and ever. Gloria in excelsis. Don't let me run off the reel.

WHITEY: I won't.

SPARKY: Please don't. If I go off then you won't have anything.

WHITEY: I can always put you on again.

SPARKY: Maybe not.

WHITEY: Maybe yes.

SPARKY: **What was happy about it? What could I celebrate that was shining?**

WHITEY: Nothing was shining.

SPARKY: **And I will always trust you because you will never disintegrate and I will never disintegrate or grate on my nerves or get on my nerves or make me nervous because I can always shut you up or turn you off.**

WHITEY: Where is everyone?

SPARKY: **They're gone but I hear footsteps. Help me, don't let them do this to me.**

WHITEY: Sparky, come down.

SPARKY: **Help me.**

WHITEY: I can't, what can I do?

SPARKY: **Help me. Don't let them do this to us. They're going to do something to us. Don't let them do this. They're coming. Stop them Whitey, stop them. There's got to be something you can do. Get me out of here. Stop the projector. Stop them. You have to stop the projector.**

WHITEY: How?

SPARKY: **Help me.**

WHITEY: I can't.

(Runs back and forth between projectors.)

SPARKY: **Stop the projector. Stop them. Do something, stop it,**

SMITH: **Whitey, don't stop it. You can't.**

WHITEY: I will.

LEE: You can't.

SPARKY: Whitey, stop the projector. Help me Whitey, the projector.

BODINE: Don't stop the projector, the film is running out.

SMITH: Let it run out Sparky.

MIRANDA: Don't let it run out Sparky. Listen to me.

SMITH: What color do you see.

SPARKY: Help me. Don't touch the projector. Let it run out. Do something.

BODINE: Whitey, turn the projector back. Turn it backward but don't turn it off.

SPARKY: Turn it off. Break it, smash it, end it. It's running out. I can see it.

SMITH: Whitey, don't. Turn it backwards. Don't do this to us.

SPARKY: Whitey, don't do it. Get me out of here.

BODINE: Listen to me Whitey.

SPARKY: Help me. Don't let them do this to me. Get me out of here. If you don't, I'll always hate you.

SMITH: Turn it back.

SPARKY: Let it run out. Stop it.

BODINE: Don't let it run out. Don't.

SPARKY: Whitey...

(Both projectors run out of film and cut SPARKY off in mid sentence. The reels spin and the screens go bright white with the

projector bulb light. This is the only light onstage.)

WHITEY: I will be dreamy and sad, dreamy and sad, always dreamy and sad for a very long time and I will last forever because I am on film and it will be my pleasure to play you over and over and over again for my pleasure and freedom and my inspiration. I will play you over and over, over again until you are shredded year after year, year after year for a thousand years, real soft and real loud whenever I want, however I can, whenever I want because after that that's all I'll be able to do, over and over again for a thousand years because that's all I'll ever know how to do by then and I'll just keep doing it and I'll just keep playing over and over again for you over and over again until I turn to shreds and when I turn to shreds you'll still hear me in your brain cavity over and over again for a thousand years and you'll always feel free because of that and even when they say I don't have a brain 1 will have a brain because I will have a brain because I do have a brain because I am a brain because the brain is right there in the plug or in your hand or in the light bulb or in the emulsion or the groove or the whatever, in the plastic for a thousand years even without electricity or whatever, over and over again because I do have a brain and I can sing if I want to because I can sing, because I can. Is that right? Do you understand me? Right? What is your name?

(WHITEY *walks across the space gently tipping over each table in his path until he reaches a projector.*)

Whitey.
You'll remember my name. What did you say?
Nothing.
That's what I thought. What is your name?
Whitey.
Whitey.
You remember my name. Always, always and forever, forever and ever. Gloria in excelsis.
Don't let me run off the reel.
I won't.
Please don't. If I go off then you won't have anything.
I can always put you on again.
Maybe not.
Maybe yes.
What was happy about it, what could I celebrate that was shining?
Nothing was shining.
And I will always trust you because you will never disintegrate and I will never disintegrate or grate on my nerves or get on my nerves or get on my nerves or make me nervous because I can always shut you up or turn you off.

Do you understand me? Do you hear me?
Do you hear me?

END

WHITE WATER

Photo credit: Massimo Agus.

WHITE WATER

Three live actors, four streams of prerecorded video, twenty monitors, six characters.
White Water was commissioned by the Institute of Contemporary Art in Boston. It was first performed there in October 1986 with the following cast:

Valerie Charles   KIRSTEN, PEGEEN
Larry Tighe   CORTEZ, DOC
Michael Tighe   MACK, PRODUCER

Text, Direction, Set and Video design: John Jesurun
Sound Design; Christian Marclay
Lighting: Jeff Nash
Technical Director: Jim Coleman
Stage Manager: Brad Phillips
Video Edit: John Jesurun, Francis Zuccarello

Setting

The playing space is rectangular, 18 feet by 36 feet. It is raked from floor level on one end to 3 feet in height at the other, and covered by an industrial gray carpet.

At each corner of the space is an upended
television monitor (19") on a black boxlike
pedestal 3 feet in height. Each of these
monitors faces inward toward the playing area.
From scene to scene talking heads appear on
these monitors, as well as various images. The
audience sits surrounding the playing space.
Surrounding the audience are 16 additional
upended monitors, each on a 15 foot pedestal.
These monitors display numerous ambient
images throughout the performance. The
image on each of the 3 main floor monitors is
duplicated so that a specific talking head can
be seen from all sides. Images and heads shift
from monitor to monitor as the piece
progresses.

The following items are preset: paper and pens
on the tables, a glass of water on the large
table, cigarettes and an ashtray on the small
table, a toreador jacket on the back of a chair.
In the text the prerecorded dialogue spoken by
the talking heads on the monitors appears in
italic type. Lines spoken live appear in roman
type.

This play was previously published in the anthology *On
New Ground:*
Contemporary Hispanic American Plays
edited by M. Elizabeth Osborne
Theatre Communications Group, New York, 1987
ISBN 0-930452-68-21(pbk.)

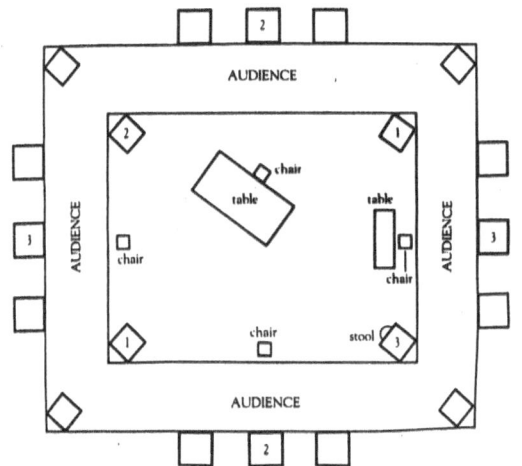

KIRSTEN sits at large table.

PRODUCER: What was that?
KIRSTEN: I saw something last night.
PRODUCER: And what was that? What was it?
KIRSTEN: I'm not sure really. It was floating
up in the sky and then it went down
into the gutter. A glowing ball.
PRODUCER: It was probably a soap bubble.
KIRSTEN: No. No it wasn't. It didn't shine like
that. It shone from the inside. *PRODUCER: OK
dear. And then what?*
KIRSTEN: Well, it disappeared.
PRODUCER: So what. Then forget about it.
KIRSTEN: I can't. I keep thinking about it.
PRODUCER: Well don't. Can we get on with this?
KIRSTEN: Who is the first guest?
PRODUCER: It's Jimmy Jam.
KIRSTEN: Jimmy Jam.
PRODUCER: The singer.
KIRSTEN: Can he talk?
PRODUCER: He can sing.
KIRSTEN: But can he talk?
PRODUCER: Probably not.
KIRSTEN: No.
*PRODUCER: Then you'll have to pre-interview
him and see if he can talk.*
KIRSTEN: And what if he can't?

PRODUCER: *If he can't talk then we make him sing a lot and then cut him off so that it* looks like we don't have any time left and he can't talk and if he can't talk then that's perfect, no love lost.

KIRSTEN: What if he can talk?

PRODUCER: *Too bad*

KIRSTEN: Too bad then. What if he wants to talk?

PRODUCER: *He's not here to talk he's here to sing Tell him that*

KIRSTEN: But he wants to talk.

PRODUCER: *How do you know that.*

KIRSTEN: All the press says that.

PRODUCER: *Then tell him we don't have enough time to talk and if he wants to talk he can talk to someone else We don't have any time to talk so tell him to talk to someone else.*

KIRSTEN: But he can sing.

PRODUCER: *So let him sing. Let him sing his heart out.*

KIRSTEN: What if he has something interesting to say?

PRODUCER: *Do you think he does?*

KIRSTEN: I think so.

PRODUCER: *Why?*

KIRSTEN: Because I've heard him talk before.

PRODUCER: *Where?*

KIRSTEN: On TV.

PRODUCER: *Do you have a tape of it?*

KIRSTEN: No, can't get one.

PRODUCER: *Do you have any print interviews of him?*

KIRSTEN: Yes, here's one or two.

PRODUCER: *What does he say?*

KIRSTEN: Read it.

PRODUCER: *I don't have any time to read it.*

KIRSTEN: Oh, there's blood on this paper, ugh, I cut myself.

PRODUCER: *Well, what does he say?*

KIRSTEN: Oh, he talks about his childhood in Ireland and all that stuff.

PRODUCER: *Anything political?*

KIRSTEN: No.

PRODUCER: *Well then that's good. Any good stories?*

KIRSTEN: Yes, once he saw a leprechaun or a holy mouse or vidi-oon or something.
It was all in the papers.

PRODUCER: *And then what happened'*

KIRSTEN: Then he didn't see it anymore and that was it. They never talked about it again.

PRODUCER: *Well, we could ask him about that.*

KIRSTEN: We don't want to get too specific, he's just a singer.

PRODUCER: *Can he sing "Danny Boy"*

KIRSTEN: Can I sing with him?

PRODUCER: *I don't think so He's pretty serious.*

KIRSTEN: If he sings, I sing. If I talk, he talks. If he doesn't talk, I talk anyway

PRODUCER: *Does he tell jokes?*

KIRSTEN: I don't know

PRODUCER: *Can he talk? Is he a talker'?*
KIRSTEN. He seems to be.
PRODUCER: *Seems isn't enough. Find out.*
KIRSTEN: He's touring in Canada or something. Find him and call him and book him tomorrow if he can talk.
PRODUCER: *What if he can't talk.*
KIRSTEN. Book him anyway. He can sing. Book him anyway. He's popular isn't he?
PRODUCER: *Oh yes, very.*
KIRSTEN: Fine, then book him anyway.
PRODUCER: *How old is he?*
KIRSTEN: Twenty-five.
PRODUCER: *Perfect age.*
KIRSTEN: For what?
PRODUCER: *For anything.*
KIRSTEN: We can ask him about the queen of England and all that.
PRODUCER: What's his name again?
KIRSTEN. Jimmy Jam.
PRODUCER: *Jimmy Jam? What kind of a name is that?*
KIRSTEN: I don't know.
PRODUCER: *Doesn't sound Irish to me.*
KIRSTEN: Did he change it? Is it a fake name?
PRODUCER: *They usually are.*
KIRSTEN: Find out. Then we can nail him with his real name.
PRODUCER: *But why?*
KIRSTEN: In case he can't talk.
PRODUCER: *Sounds like a fake name.*

KIRSTEN: Isn't Bob Dylan a fake name?

PRODUCER: *We'll talk about Bob Dylan first and then...*

KIRSTEN: Nail him with his fake name.

PRODUCER: *Did you get all that?*

KIRSTEN: Yes.

PRODUCER: *Anything else?*

KIRSTEN: Anyone else?

PRODUCER: *There's the bishop and the mayor of Constantinople.*

KIRSTEN: Cancel the mayor. I don't think that'll be interesting.

PRODUCER: *He can talk. He can really talk*

KIRSTEN: Who cares. Does he have anything interesting to say?

PRODUCER: *Probably not.*

KIRSTEN: Who else?

PRODUCER: *Tina Turner, Irene Dunne and Marie Curie*

KIRSTEN: I thought she was dead?

PRODUCER: *So did I*

KIRSTEN: She's alive.

PRODUCER: *I can't bear the sight of another movie star and their stupid stories about the shores of Babylon.*

KIRSTEN: Book her.

PRODUCER: *Can I finish telling you what I saw last night?*

KIRSTEN: No, that's it. Call me tomorrow with the results.

PRODUCER: *Resultata Go, you are dismissed, go in peace.*

KIRSTEN: Thanks be to God.

(Cut)

MACK seated. *KIRSTEN and DOC at tables. On monitors, daytime shot of window full of light.*

MACK: 1 know you're going to be upset but I know what I'm saying. It's the truth and I don't mean maybe.

PRODUCER: *And what is it exactly that you saw?*

MACK: First I saw a light in the sky.

PEGEEN: *Flashing?*

MACK: Like a cigarette glowing in the dark except it was daylight.

DOC: Was it an angel or something?

MACK: Oh no it wasn't an angel it was something better.

KIRSTEN: How do you know it wasn't the devil trying to trick you?

MACK: Trick me into what?

PRODUCER: *Trick you into thinking you saw something incredible.*

MACK: Why would he do that?

DOC: To confuse you. Lead you on the wrong path so he could destroy you.

MACK: No.

PEGEEN: *Do you see these things often?*

MACK: No.

KIRSTEN: Have you ever seen anything like this before?

MACK: Never. DOC: Have you ever had a daydream that was so strong you thought it was really happening?

MACK: I never daydream I only see what's there. If it isn't there I don't see it. If I don't see it it's not there and that's why I'm sure that I saw this and that it was really there and if I saw it, it was really there.

PEGEEN: *Doesn't it seem foolish to you7*

PRODUCER: *Had you been reading any religious comic books or anything?*

MACK: No.

KIRSTEN: Have you ever read the Bible or anything which could be of any influence to what you saw?

MACK: No, I never read anything religious.

DOC: Have you been seeing any religious programs on TV?

MACK: No.

PEGEEN: *Have you ever seen any of them?*

PRODUCER: *Which ones?*

MACK: I don't know, they're all the same to me.

KIRSTEN: Do you watch them often?

MACK: No, I just saw a few by mistake when I was switching channels.

DOC: So you think they could have influenced you into seeing anything?

MACK: No, because those people don't really see anything like this.

PEGEEN: *What do you think of these shows?*

PRODUCER: You don't think anything at all about them' You don't have any feelings about them?

MACK: No, not at all.

KIRSTEN: Were you brought up religiously?

MACK: No.

DOC: Did your parents ever have you memorize any prayers?

MACK: One or two.

PEGEEN: *Which ones?*

MACK: Our Father.

PRODUCER: *Can you repeat it?*

MACK: Our Father who art in heaven, hallowed by thy name. Thy kingdom come, thy will be done on earth as it is in heaven. Give us this day our daily bread and forgive us our trespasses as we forgive those who trespass against us and lead us not into temptation but deliver us from evil. For thine is the power and the kingdom and the glory now and forever. Amen.

KIRSTEN: What do you think of that prayer?

MACK: Nothing really.

DOC: Do you believe it?

MACK: Not really.

PEGEEN: *Do you think there is a God?*

PRODUCER: *Why?*

MACK: I just don't think there is anything there.

KIRSTEN: Did anyone tell you this?

MACK: No.

DOC: Do you talk about God much with other people?

MACK: No, the subject never comes up.

PEGEEN Are you interested m God?

MACK: No.

PRODUCER: *What exactly do you think this thing is that you saw' Something from outer space?*

MACK: Maybe.

KIRSTEN. But not a God.

MACK: Maybe. It might be, but not a Bible God.

DOC:. If it's not a Bible God then what kind of God could it be?

MACK: Something from the sky or universe.

KIRSTEN: A form of energy?

PEGEEN: *A form of energy.*

PRODUCER: *How do you know you just didn't experience it in your mind?*

MACK: Because I know I saw it.

KIRSTEN: But no one else saw it.

MACK: I know they didn't see it but it really is there.

DOC: How can you explain the fact that no one else saw it and you did?

MACK: Because I've seen it a few times already and it's speaking to me.

PEGEEN: *It?*

MACK: She.

PRODUCER: *Who is she?*

MACK: We've gone through this before. I don't know.

KIRSTEN: Do you listen to a lot of loud music?

MACK: Sort of.

DOC: What kind?

MACK: Just what's on the radio.

PEGEEN Do you have earphones?

PRODUCER: Do you play them very loud?

MACK: Sometimes.

KIRSTEN: Do you think that you had them on when you experienced this vision?

MACK: It wasn't a vision, she was there.

DOC: Now we have a transcript of what she said.

PEGEEN. And she doesn't say much.

MACK: She's the quiet type I guess.

KIRSTEN: Do you believe in the devil?

MACK: No.

DOC: Do you think the devil might have had anything to do with this?

MACK: I don't believe in the devil.

PEGEEN. What do you think the devil is?

MACK: The devil is what people think is bad and they think it's a person that is
personified in all this evil and tempts them to do bad things so they can blame
all the bad things on the devil.

PRODUCER: Have you ever been in a Catholic church?

MACK: No

KIRSTEN: Have you ever seen pictures of a Catholic church7

MACK: No

DOC: Have you ever seen pictures of saints or God in books?

PEGEEN: *Did they look anything like what you saw?*

MACK: Not at all.

PRODUCER: *Can you explain why?*

KIRSTEN: Compare what you saw to what we can see in a book.

MACK: In a book they use colors that look very pretty and these colors around her aren't really colors, they're light and I can't really see her face so clearly and she's not wearing clothes and she's not particularly any size or body shape and she's not holding a rosary or a cross or anything like that and she's not floating on a cloud and there aren't angels around or flowers and she's not always looking up into the sky.

DOC: Does she wear shoes?

MACK: I told you she wasn't wearing anything

PEGEEN: *Do you ever look at magazines like Playboy?*

PRODUCER: *Does she look like anything in those magazines?*

MACK: No.

KIRSTEN: If she's not wearing any clothes there must be some resemblance.

DOC: Or similarity.

MACK: No similarity.

PEGEEN: *How do you know she's a woman?*

MACK: She sounds like a woman. She has a

woman's voice and face.

PRODUCER: *But she doesn't really have any bodily features that show she's a woman.*

MACK: She doesn't really have a body like that. I told you.

KIRSTEN: Just tell us what she looks like in simple terms as simply as you can

DOC: If you can't come up with a clear description how can we believe you?

PEGEEN: *It just sounds like you're making it all up.*

MACK: I'm not.

PRODUCER: *That's why we have to have as clear of a description as we can so that it will be acceptable to the other people, otherwise....*

KIRSTEN: They'll think you're making it all up.

MACK: You keep asking me all these questions over and over again. Why is the lawyer here?

PEGEEN: *I have to be. We don't want to step on anyone's toes.*

MACK: Have I ever given the wrong answer? Have I ever contradicted myself?

DOC: No, not yet.

PEGEEN: *How many people have been cured'*

MACK: Twenty-five or thirty.

PRODUCER: *And why is this?*

MACK: I don't know why.

KIRSTEN: And why do you think this is?

MACK: I don't know.

DOC: Surely you must know something.

PEGEEN: *Here you saw this woman and told a few people.*

PRODUCER: *And they followed you but didn't see her.*

KIRSTEN: And some people who were sick got it into their heads that this was something supernatural and several were cured.

DOC: And now several have turned into many.

PEGEEN: *Surely you must think there is some connection.*

PRODUCER: *There is a connection isn't there?*

MACK: Yes.

KIRSTEN: Has the woman admitted curing all these people?

MACK: Not really.

DOC: What does she think about all of this?

MACK: She doesn't talk about it.

PEGEEN: *What does she talk about?*

MACK: She just asks me to come back and pray.

PRODUCER: *What kind of prayers?*

KIRSTEN: Any prayers that you know already?

MACK: No.

DOC: Does she give you a certain prayer to say?

MACK: No, she says to pray however I want.

PEGEEN: *Do you pray to her?*

MACK: She says not to pray to her.

PRODUCER: *Do you think she's a god?*

MACK: Not really.

KIRSTEN: Is she working for another god?

MACK: I don't think so.

DOC: Is she from another planet?

MACK: I don't think so.

PEGEEN: *Why won't she tell you who she is?*

MACK: She doesn't think it matters.

PRODUCER: *What do you pray about, who do you pray to, who do you pray for?* MACK: I just pray for everyone.

KIRSTEN: But when you pray are you just making wishes or asking someone or something in particular to do something?

DOC: Do you think this woman is dead or a ghost?

MACK: I don't really believe in ghosts.

PEGEEN: *Where do you think people go to when they die?*

MACK: Into the ground.

PRODUCER: *And that's it.*

MACK: That's it.

KIRSTEN: No heaven, no hell.

MACK: Right.

DOC: If she told you there was a heaven and hell would you believe her?

MACK: Maybe.

PEGEEN: *So you wouldn't necessarily believe everything she told you?*

MACK: No.

PRODUCER: *Do you think she'd mind or stop coming if you didn't believe what she told you?*

MACK: Well I might believe what she told me and I might not. The one thing I do believe is that she's there.

KIRSTEN: What do the people who are cured and come to pray believe?

MACK: I don't know what they believe or who they believe in.

DOC: Who are they praying to?

MACK: I never ask them but I think they're saying all kinds of Bible prayers.

PEGEEN: *Have any priests come?*

MACK: A lot.

PRODUCER: *And what do they say?*

MACK: They ask me the same questions you do and I tell them the same answers.

KIRSTEN: Do they want certain answers?

MACK: Yes, they want a connection to what they believe in.

DOC: Do they get it?

MACK: They make it up if they can but I tell them there isn't.

PEGEEN: *What do your friends think about this?*

MACK: Some don't talk to me because their parents think I'm crazy. Others come with me and try to see her but they don't and they get mad because they can't see her.

PRODUCER: *What do you tell them?*

MACK: I tell them to keep looking.

KIRSTEN: Do they wonder why they can't see her and you can?

MACK: Yes, but I can't explain it to them.

DOC: Do they think that you're special or a better person because you can see her and they can't?

MACK: Sometimes.

PEGEEN: *Do you still have the same relationship with them that you did before?*

MACK: No, I really don't have any friends now because they think I've changed.

PRODUCER: *Do you think you've changed?*

MACK: Yes.

KIRSTEN: How do you think you've changed?

MACK: Well, I see this person and I'm much calmer now than I used to be and instead of playing and listening to music I pray or go out to the water.

DOC: Do you like the water?

MACK: Sure.

PEGEEN: *Have you always liked the water?*

MACK: Yes.

PRODUCER: *Can you swim?*

MACK: No.

KIRSTEN: Don't you think you should learn?

MACK: I should but I'm afraid of the water.

DOC: Afraid of drowning?

PEGEEN: *Where do you think all this will lead?*

MACK: I don't know, I guess more people will get cured.

PRODUCER: *And what will happen to you?*

MACK: I'll just keep seeing her until she goes away.

KIRSTEN: Do you think she'll go away
eventually and people will stop being cured?
MACK: Probably, this can't go on forever.
DOC: Why not?
MACK: It doesn't seem right.
PEGEEN: *Why not?*
MACK: Well, it could get out of hand.
PRODUCER: *If she said she would keep coming
back and you would have to pray to her
for the rest of your life would you do it?*
MACK: I guess so.
KIRSTEN: If she asked you to make a church
and bring people there would you do it?
MACK: I think so.
DOC: Do you think you're an interesting
person or a dull person?
PEGEEN: *What do the parents say?*
MACK: They're very upset. They don't want to
let me go to the water and pray.
PRODUCER: *And what do you do?*
MACK: I sneak out.
KIRSTEN: You disobey them.
MACK: I have to. She wants me to come and
talk to her.
DOC: So you do whatever she tells you.
PEGEEN: *Do all these people and attention make
you nervous?*
MACK: A little.
PRODUCER: *You seem very calm.*
KIRSTEN: Are you?
MACK: Yes.

DOC: If you went on TV would you be nervous?

PEGEEN: *Do you want to go on TV?*

MACK: Not really.

PRODUCER: *Why not?*

MACK: I just don't want to. I wouldn't like it.

KIRSTEN: Why not?

MACK: I don't like television.

PEGEEN: *Does it glow the same way she glows?*

MACK: No.

PRODUCER: *What's the difference between the glow?*

MACK: She glows but she's not plugged in.

KIRSTEN: If she asked you to go on TV would you?

MACK: Yes.

DOC: So she isn't a god?

MACK: Probably not.

PEGEEN: *But if she eventually told you she was a god you would believe her.*

MACK: Maybe.

KIRSTEN: Do you want her to be a god?

MACK: No.

DOC: Why?

MACK: I just don't. I'm not interested in that.

PEGEEN: *But if she said she was a god and she was curing all these people wouldn't you accept her as that?*

MACK: I guess I'd have to but I'd rather she not be a god.

PRODUCER: *Why?*

MACK: Who needs it?

KIRSTEN: I don't think your answers are particularly enlightening. They seem honest but they don't shed any great light on the subject.

DOC: You seem to be the tool of someone.

PEGEEN: *He just is too young to really understand all this completely.*

DOC: He has an intuitive understanding.

PRODUCER: *He has an intuitive understanding.*

PEGEEN: *You don't think this is a UFO do you?*

MACK: No.

PRODUCER: *Have you ever heard of stories of people who have been taken up in flying saucers and had experiences?*

MACK: Yes.

KIRSTEN: And so you don't think that's happening here?

MACK: No.

DOC: Why?

MACK: I don't see a spaceship but it might be.

PEGEEN: *Are you worried that people might think you're a fake?*

MACK: But I never said anything to mislead anyone, no one.

PRODUCER: *Yes but...*

MACK: No but.

KIRSTEN: Do you know how your parents died?

MACK: Yes in a car crash.

DOC: The day you were born. Do you think that means anything?

MACK: Do you mean psycho?

PEGEEN: *Yes.*

MACK: No.

PRODUCER: *Are you angry at God for it?*

MACK: No, he didn't do it.

KIRSTEN: But he may have let it happen.

MACK: He didn't let it happen, they were both drunk.

DOC: So that's that.

MACK: They did it to themselves.

PEGEEN: *And then you went to live with your aunt.*

MACK: Yes.

PRODUCER: *Had she seen anything,*

MACK: Anything what?

KIRSTEN: Any visions or ladies?

MACK: No.

DOC: Was she odd?

PEGEEN: *Was she sort of nutty at all?*

MACK: No, not until all this started happening.

PRODUCER: *Who saw things first?*

MACK: I did and then when I told her about all of them she started seeing things pretty soon after.

KIRSTEN: Why?

MACK: I don't know why.

DOC: Is she seeing things?

PEGEEN: *Do you believe her?*

MACK: Sort of.

PRODUCER: *Sort of yes or sort of no?*

MACK: Sort of yes.

KIRSTEN: Do you think she might be lying?

PEGEEN: *Maybe?*

KIRSTEN: Maybe?

PRODUCER: *Does he think you're lying to him?*

MACK: No.

KIRSTEN: He believed you right from the start.

MACK: Yes.

PEGEEN: *And why do you think he started seeing things?*

MACK: I think because his wife died a few years ago.

DOC: I see.

PRODUCER: *And maybe he's flipping out.*

KIRSTEN: Way out. MACK: Pretty far out.

DOC: What do you think that means?

PEGEEN: *If we know what it means then the information has value to us in understanding this.*

MACK: Understand and incinerate, incarcerate.

DOC: Understand and incinerate?

PRODUCER: *Do you find that symbolic?*

MACK: I hate symbols.

(Cut)

MACK sits on stool, speaks to monitor across diagonal. River scene on ambient monitors.

DOC: *Well my child, are you feeling sick?*

MACK: Yes sir, doctor.

DOC: *What's the matter?*

MACK: I'm having trouble with my chest.
DOC: *Are we making you tired?*
MACK: Oh, no ma'am I can talk all right today.
DOC: *Don't you drink the water from the spring?*
MACK: Sure.
DOC: *That water cures other sick people, why doesn't it cure you?*
MACK: Maybe the lady wants me to suffer.
DOC: *Why does she want you to suffer?*
MACK: Oh, because I need it.
DOC: *And why do you need it instead of other people?*
MACK: I don't know.
DOC: *Do you still go to the cliff?*
MACK: I go there when the police let me.
DOC: *Why doesn't the police commissioner let you go there when ever…*
MACK: …you want.
DOC: *Because everyone keeps following me.*
MACK: But they say that you've gone there even though you'd been…
DOC: *…forbidden.*
MACK: Yes sir.
DOC: *And why have you stopped going there?*
MACK: Because before I felt a strong urge to go and I couldn't hold myself back.
DOC: *And now you don't feel the urge?*
MACK: No.
DOC: *Suppose you got the urge like before, would you go back?*
MACK: Yes I would.

DOC: *Did the lady tell you what you had to do to get to heaven?*

MACK: No, everyone knows what they have to do.

DOC: *Did she talk to you often?*

MACK: Yes.

DOC: *Every time?*

MACK: No, not every time.

DOC: *What are you doing?*

MACK: I have to wash my eyes.

DOC: *Why?*

MACK: I can't see very well with them, I can't read so well with them.

DOC: *Why is that?*

MACK: I don't know.

DOC: *Have you had trouble with your eyes before?*

MACK: No.

DOC: *What is wrong with them exactly?*

MACK: I can't read so well, it's hard to read the letters so well.

DOC: *Have you gone to the doctor?*

MACK: Yes.

DOC: *And what does he say to do?*

MACK: He can't really explain it. He just says that I'm gradually seeing less well. I think my eyes are somehow getting smaller and letting less light into them.

DOC: *Do you think you're going blind?*

MACK: Yes.

DOC: *Why can't you get cured?*

MACK: I don't know.

DOC: *Have you asked her to help you?*
MACK: Yes.
DOC: *And what does she say?*
MACK: She says I must continue on and that if I go blind it must…
DOC: *…be the way it must be.*
MACK: And if that must be the way it must be….don't you think?
DOC : *That's cruel of her not to help you.*
MACK: No.
DOC: *But she can help you. Why doesn't she?*
MACK: She doesn't because it just has to be that way. That is the way the groove is cut for my life.
DOC: *Did she tell you that?*
MACK: She said that.
DOC: *And you believe that.*
MACK: I believe that.
DOC: *Are people praying for you?*
MACK: Yes.
DOC: *And why won't it help?*
MACK: Some things just won't. That's what she told me and I must accept it.
 DOC: Are you lying to me?
MACK: No.
DOC: Are you lying to me?
MACK: No.
DOC: *If you were lying to me would you tell me?*
MACK: I would tell you if I was lying.
DOC: *Can you see the horizon from here?*
MACK: Yes.

DOC: *What does it look like?*
MACK: It looks like a black line.
DOC: *That's what you see. Do you want to know what 1 see?*
MACK: Yes.
DOC: *Do you want to know what 1 see? I'll tell what I see. On the horizon is a row of hills and rocks and the sun behind it. Why do you think your uncle brought you here?* MACK: He wants me to stop seeing all these things.
DOC: *Do you think you'll ever stop seeing these things?*
MACK: Eventually.
DOC: *Did she tell you that?*
MACK: Yes.
DOC: *Do you think that Mrs. X is seeing things at the spring too'?*
MACK: Near a tree.
DOC: *Oh yes that's right. Do you think she sees them?*
MACK: Sure.
DOC: *So she sees them and you see them.*
MACK: We both see them.
DOC: *Are they the same things?*
MACK: I don't know.
DOC: *You don't know.*
MACK: How would I know?
DOC: *I don't know why. Wouldn't you know?*
MACK: Because she has her eyes and I have my eyes.
DOC: *We'll stop now you're tired.*

(Cut)

MACK in chair, PEGEEN at large table, CORTEZ pacing. On monitors, closeups of hands writing.

KIRSTEN: And who are you?
CORTEZ: A lawyer and a priest.
KIRSTEN: In that order?
CORTEZ: No order particularly.
PRODUCER: What religion?
CORTEZ: No particular religion.
PRODUCER: Let me see if I understand this. This young man was your altar boy and now you are testifying against him to prevent him from being interviewed on this television show.
CORTEZ: And who are you?
PRODUCER: The executive producer.
CORTEZ: Yes. I'm trying to get him to understand that he seems to have hallucinated something and that in itself isn't wrong but it's not something that should be spoken about on television.
PEGEEN: And why is that?
CORTEZ: Because I don't think it's true. As a matter of fact it'll all pass.
KIRSTEN: Do you think the boy is a hysteric?
CORTEZ: This could push him into it.
PRODUCER: And what qualifies you to say that?
CORTEZ: I've known him for a while.

KIRSTEN: *And has he shown evidence of hysteria-poisoning in or outside of the church? Tell the truth.*

CORTEZ: Not particularly but he has a healthy imagination.

PEGEEN: Is it healthier than yours?

CORTEZ: I don't think that's at issue here.

PRODUCER: *Then what is?*

CORTEZ: His connection with the cures is not altogether convincing.

KIRSTEN: *Why?*

CORTEZ: It just hasn't happened like that historically.

PEGEEN: But he hasn't said the apparitions are affiliated with your church.

CORTEZ: Exactly.

PRODUCER: *Would you like them to be?*

CORTEZ: Obviously not.

KIRSTEN: *Why is it so important that he not be interviewed?*

CORTEZ: Because we do not want any associations whatsoever.

PEGEEN: But you can disclaim, disown.

CORTEZ: We can but we don't want to go so far as to create a disturbance in our community.

PRODUCER: *How far do you want to go?*

CORTEZ: Not very far.

KIRSTEN: *Would you also like to be on the show?*

CORTEZ: No I wouldn't.

PEGEEN: Why?

CORTEZ: I told you I don't want to make a big stink about it all right?

PRODUCER: *But you're doing that right now.*

CORTEZ: I'm making a big stink now so that we won't have to make a bigger one later.

KIRSTEN: *If we go on with this show will your parish be upset?*

CORTEZ: Extremely.

PEGEEN: Why do you wear that thing?

MACK: What thing?

PRODUCER: *That black thing.*

MACK: I always wear it, she told me to wear it.

KIRSTEN: *She, who?*

CORTEZ: She, the lady of the lake or who?

MACK: The lady I saw by the water.

PEGEEN: Do you wear it to the beach?

MACK: Yes.

PEGEEN: Isn't it hot?

MACK: Yes.

CORTEZ: He took it from the sacristy and I'd appreciate it if he'd return it.

MACK: I did return it. This is mine I bought it.

PRODUCER: *Did you like serving mass?*

MACK: Yes.

KIRSTEN: *How many times did you serve mass?*

MACK: Exactly once.

PEGEEN: Why?

MACK: I dropped the Bible and they threw me out.

PRODUCER: *Is that true?*

CORTEZ: Not exactly.

KIRSTEN: *Well what happened, did he drop the book?*

CORTEZ: Yes.

PEGEEN: *And what happened?*

CORTEZ: He was asked to leave.

MACK: Same thing.

PRODUCER: *And so you think because he's a disaffected altar boy he's now running out and seeing his own thing so to speak and competing with you.*

CORTEZ: Partially.

KIRSTEN: *But how does that explain the cures?*

CORTEZ: It doesn't.

PEGEEN: *Do you have an explanation?*

CORTEZ: No.

PRODUCER: *Are you sure you don't have one up your sleeve?*

KIRSTEN: *Someone hiding somewhere with a great story about them?*

CORTEZ: No, we do not. We're just trying to be as cautious and fair about this as possible.

PEGEEN: *Why don't you believe him?*

CORTEZ: He's young and imaginative.

PRODUCER: *But everyone does.*

CORTEZ: That's just it. It's too easy.

KIRSTEN: *And you don't think this is connected with your church or any doctrines in your church?*

MACK: But we missed something.

PEGEEN: *What?*

MACK: I was never really an altar boy. I never went to church. My cousin Jimmy Riley was sick and so he told me what to do and I went in for him because he said he'd catch hellfire if he didn't go in so I went in for him and it wasn't till I dropped the book that he noticed I wasn't Jimmy Riley.

KIRSTEN: *So that was the only time you were in a church.*

MACK: Right.

PRODUCER: *But Jimmy Riley must have told you things about the church so that you must know more than a little.*

MACK: I know a little more than a little but not much else.

KIRSTEN: *Do you want to have your own church someday?*

MACK: No, I don't want to have anything, I just saw this person, she started talking to me and then the spring started and then people followed me and started getting cured and everyone started to flip out.

PEGEEN: Do you feel holy?

MACK: Not at all.

PRODUCER: *Where are your parents?*

MACK: In Tibet.

CORTEZ: Tibet?

KIRSTEN *What are they doing in Tibet?*

MACK: Second honeymoon.

PEGEEN: Can't you call them?

PRODUCER:. *They're riding camels somewhere in Mongolia.*

CORTEZ: You pulled this stunt Mack Riley just when they left just to get attention why don't you just admit it.

PRODUCER: *Beat it.*

CORTEZ: How could you do something like this? It's deplorable.

PRODUCER: *Beat it.*

MACK: You're just jealous because I got all these miracles and you've been trying your whole life for one and you still didn't get one.

CORTEZ: Deplorable.

KIRSTEN: *It's never too late.*

PEGEEN: What religion are your parents?

MACK: None I told you.

PRODUCER: *Do you believe in God?*

MACK: No.

KIRSTEN: *So what the hell do you think you're seeing if you're not seeing God or one of his minions?*

MACK: I keep telling you I don't even know what I'm seeing but I saw it and I saw it and those people got cured.

PEGEEN: They did get cured.

CORTEZ: They say they did.

KIRSTEN: *So does everyone else. And then there's the dog. How did that dead dog come to life?*

PEGEEN: How many people have reported cures to the Environmental Protection Agency?

PRODUCER: *Seven hundred and twenty-five as of today.*

KIRSTEN: *And what are the cures?*

PEGEEN: Cancer, broken legs, AIDS, terminal spinal meningitis.

CORTEZ: They're all lunatics and hysterics.

PRODUCER: *What is the name of your church?*

CORTEZ: The South Lawn Invitational Congregation.

KIRSTEN: *And what is that? Forgive me is that Catholic?*

CORTEZ: No it's not.

PEGEEN: Is it affiliated with a larger confraternity of beliefs?

CORTEZ: Not formally

PRODUCER: *Did you go to divinity school?*

CORTEZ: Yes, Harvard and Yale.

KIRSTEN: *Do you know the Pope at all?*

CORTEZ: Of course not.

PEGEEN: Just checking.

CORTEZ: This is all a perversion of everything.

PRODUCER: *What are the cures if they're not miraculous?*

KIRSTEN: *Explain that.*

CORTEZ: I can't explain it.

PEGEEN: Well, there you go.

CORTEZ: And you're going to hell young man.

KIRSTEN: *See you there.*

PEGEEN: Lighten up.

CORTEZ: I will not lighten up.

PRODUCER: *You're getting hysterical.*

KIRSTEN: *Would you come on the show if he goes on?*

CORTEZ: No.

PEGEEN: Why not? You could counteract him, defame him, retaliate, clear the air, make your point.

CORTEZ: I don't want to be immodest.

PEGEEN: Okay.

PRODUCER: He'll have to go on alone.

KIRSTEN Are you sure?

CORTEZ: I don't want to make a big stink I said.

PRODUCER:. You're inflating this out of proportion.

KIRSTEN: He's just another guest of interest to the audience.

CORTEZ: This is all typical of the disintegration of life on this planet because of people like you.

(Cut)

MACK in a different chair, KIRSTEN at small table.

PEGEEN: And so what if it is?

CORTEZ: I want to ask you one thing, can I?

KIRSTEN: Go ahead.

CORTEZ- When you were walking, where did you say you were walking?

MACK: I was walking where I was walking, along the riverbank.

CORTEZ: Along the riverbank. Was there sand'

MACK: No.

CORTEZ: Rocks?

MACK: Rocks and stones.

CORTEZ: *Rocks and stones, I see. And then in your own words what did you see?*

MACK: Well, I saw a glowing thing.

CORTEZ: *What kind of glowing thing?*

MACK: A ball floating in the sky.

CORTEZ: *What color was it?*

MACK: Red or blue.

CORTEZ: *Red or blue but not either one?*

MACK: Sometimes it was red or blue or yellow.

CORTEZ: *And then what?*

MACK: Then that was it.

CORTEZ: *That was it. That was the first time you saw it.*

MACK: That was the first time I saw it.

CORTEZ: *And when was the second time you saw it?*

MACK: The next day.

CORTEZ: *I thought you said it was the next week.*

MACK: I said it was the next week.

PRODUCER: *The records say the next week.*

CORTEZ: *Why didn't you see it the next day?*

MACK: 1 don't know.

CORTEZ: *Did you go there the next day?*

MACK: Yes.

CORTEZ: *And why didn't you see it?*

MACK: Because it wasn't there or maybe it was there.

CORTEZ: *Maybe it was there and you just didn't see it.*

MACK: Or it didn't show itself to me.

CORTEZ: *What are you talking about when you mean it?*

MACK: It. I mean the glowing ball.

CORTEZ: *At this point it was just a glowing ball?*

MACK: At this point it was just a glowing ball.

PEGEEN: *Objection. He's putting words in his mouth.*

CORTEZ: *I am putting words in his mouth.*

PRODUCER: *Overruled.*

KIRSTEN: So at this point it was just a glowing ball.

CORTEZ: *And then what?*

MACK: Then it was a glowing ball.

CORTEZ: *Purple and…*

MACK: …red and blue, sometimes yellow.

CORTEZ: *I see. How big was it?*

MACK: About this big.

CORTEZ: *This big?*

MACK: No, this big.

CORTEZ: *And then what?*

MACK: I told you.

CORTEZ: *Then.*

MACK: What?

CORTEZ: *Nothing?*

MACK: What?

CORTEZ: *So then you didn't see it the next week.*

MACK: I saw it the next week but not the next day.

CORTEZ: *But it was there?*

MACK: Oh yes, I know it was there.

CORTEZ: *Why didn't it show itself to you when it was* there?

MACK: It didn't want to.

CORTEZ: *Why didn't it want to?*

KIRSTEN: Who the fuck knows or cares?

PRODUCER: *I must ask for some restraint.*

PEGEEN: *Restrain Kirsten.*

CORTEZ: *So this glowing basketball.*

MACK: It wasn't a basketball.

PEGEEN: *Glowing ball.*

CORTEZ: *Glowing ball. Was it a meatball, a butterball, a football, a baseball?*

MACK: Fireball.

CORTEZ: *A fireball. And then the next day…*

MACK: Week.

CORTEZ: *Week.*

MACK: What did you see? I saw something inside it.

CORTEZ: *Something or someone?*

MACK: Someone.

CORTEZ: *A person, a child, a dog, a what?*

MACK: First I thought it was a child.

CORTEZ: *A child inside the ball.*

MACK: How big was it then?

CORTEZ: *The same size but this time it got bigger as it came to me.*

MACK: It came toward you?

CORTEZ: *Yes, from very far away on the horizon. And then what? Did it give you a message?*

MACK: No, it just said hello.

CORTEZ: *You say it. What is it? A child, a man, a woman, a dog, a horse, a robot, a teabag?*

MACK: It was a person.

CORTEZ: *Man woman or child?*

MACK: Child.

CORTEZ: *Man or woman?*

MACK: A woman.

CORTEZ: *What kind of woman?*

MACK: A nice woman.

CORTEZ: *What language did she speak?*

MACK: No language.

CORTEZ: *Well, was it English?*

MACK: No.

CORTEZ: *Latin?*

MACK: No, she didn't speak any language I knew but I understand her.

CORTEZ: *And when she came toward you how big did she get?*

MACK: About as big as you are inside the ball.

CORTEZ: *And what color was the ball?*

MACK: No color.

CORTEZ: *Now it's no color.*

MACK: No color.

CORTEZ: *Did she have a wand or anything?*

MACK: No.

CORTEZ: *Was she wearing wings or anything?*

MACK: No.

CORTEZ: *What was she wearing?*

MACK: Nothing.

CORTEZ: *She was naked?*

MACK: I didn't say that.

CORTEZ: *She was wearing nothing you said. She had to be naked.*

MACK: No she didn't.

CORTEZ: *So here you are seeing naked women in colorless basketballs in the sky.*

MACK: No basketball. no naked women and…

CORTEZ: *Have you ever seen…*

MACK: No.

CORTEZ: *1 didn't finish. What was she wearing?*

MACK: Nothing I said.

CORTEZ: *Well, if she wasn't wearing anything, what did her body look like?*

MACK: Just light.

CORTEZ: *Light-colored?*

MACK: No, just light.

CORTEZ: *Well, did you see breasts, did she have breasts?*

MACK: No. I didn't and she didn't.

CORTEZ: *So she was just floating there wearing no clothes.*

MACK: Well I didn't see any clothes but she just had light around
her.

CORTEZ: *Well, if she wasn't wearing clothes then you must have* seen her body and if didn't see her body then she must have been wearing clothes.

MACK: Wrong. She just had light around her.

KIRSTEN: Okay. We'll accept that.

PRODUCER: *Thank you dear.*

CORTEZ: *Have you ever seen The Wizard of Oz?*

MACK: What's that?

CORTEZ: *A movie.*

MACK: What is it about?

CORTEZ: *It's about a little girl who sees a woman in a floating ball*

MACK: No, I've never seen it.

CORTEZ: *Are you sure?*

MACK: Do you know who Judy Garland is?

CORTEZ: *Yes. How can you know who Judy Garland is and not have seen The Wizard of Oz? Everyone sees it.*

MACK: I didn't.

CORTEZ: *Did you read it?*

MACK: No.

CORTEZ: *What did the woman say?*

MACK: Nothing at first.

CORTEZ: *So she said nothing, she wore nothing and when she spoke she spoke in an unintelligible, unrecognizable language that you understood.*

MACK: Right.

CORTEZ: *Could I understand it if she spoke to me?*

MACK: No, because she wouldn't speak to you.

CORTEZ: *Why wouldn't she speak to me?*

MACK: First of all you wouldn't be able to see or hear her.

CORTEZ: *Why?*

MACK: She only comes to me.

CORTEZ: *Why?*

MACK: Because she only likes me.

CORTEZ: *Why?*

MACK: Because 1 can see her.

CORTEZ: *Why?*

MACK: Because she only shows herself to me.

CORTEZ: *Why, could anyone else see her?*

MACK: Maybe.

CORTEZ: *Maybe but not really.*

MACK: Maybe.

CORTEZ: *So she only comes to you.*

PEGEEN: *And you're the only one that sees her.*

CORTEZ: *If you're the only one that sees her then how do you know she's there?*

MACK: Because I see her.

CORTEZ: *What did she say?*

MACK: She sang first.

CORTEZ: *What did she sing?*

MACK: She sang this strange song.

CORTEZ: *Can you remember it or were you in too much of a psychedelic delirium to remember it.*

MACK: Actually it's hard to remember, it was a very complicated chord change. It sort of goes like this.

(*MACK sings the melody from "Au fond du Temple Saint" from Bizet's "The Pearl Fishers" a cappella, using "la la" in place of the words. He sings out of tune for a minute until CORTEZ interrupts him.*

CORTEZ: *Was there background music?*

MACK: No.

CORTEZ: *A cappella?*

MACK: A cappella.

CORTEZ: *Were there words to the song?*

MACK: No, she was just singing.

CORTEZ: *Was her voice high or low?*

KIRSTEN: This is ridiculous.

CORTEZ: *It is not.*

KIRSTEN: Can I continue for a while, maybe I can shed some light. So she sang a song and then what happened?

CORTEZ: *He was astonished, beatified, wonderized, at peak altitude. "Oh Godzilla!" he thought, "What is this?"*

PEGEEN: *Don't start up.*

DOC: What did she say Mack?

MACK: She said hello.

CORTEZ: *Was she white?*

MACK: No color really.

CORTEZ: *Well, did she have white....*

(Cut)

(CORTEZ paces.)

DOC: *Let's put it this way, could she be related to you? I mean did she have features like yours or mine or his?*

MACK: She looked like anyone.

PEGEEN: Was she beautiful?

MACK: Not in that way.

CORTEZ: Well in what way?

MACK: Not in any way.

DOC: What color were her eyes?

MACK: She didn't have any eyes, she said they were burnt out, and that I had to help her get them back.

DOC: And did you?

MACK: Yes.

DOC: And how did you do that?

CORTEZ: This is where the robbery comes in.

MACK: She said they were washed away.

KIRSTEN: By what?

MACK: By the mountain of mud and the sound, the noise of mud curdling in the mountain of mud that came up to here.

CORTEZ: This is where the robbery comes in.

KIRSTEN: What robbery?

CORTEZ: The eyes that you stole from the statue in the cathedral.

MACK: I didn't steal them.

CORTEZ: Then where are they? Who took them?

MACK: She said they were her eyes and so I gave them back to her.

CORTEZ: He stole those eyes and they are quite valuable. Do you know what those eyes are made out of?

MACK: Some kind of quartz.

CORTEZ: A very expensive quartz.

KIRSTEN: Can she see now?

MACK: She can.

PEGEEN: Did she have any message?

MACK: No.

KIRSTEN: *Can you repeat what it was she said to you in the order that she said it?*

MACK: Yes.

PEGEEN: Repeat the entire conversation. The first conversation you had with her.

MACK: The first time I talked to her.

KIRSTEN: *Yes.*

MACK: Well, she said hello- first she sang.

CORTEZ: Yes, we know she sang some stupid song.

MACK: It wasn't a stupid song. Then I said hello, then she said…

PEGEEN: In her own words.

MACK: She said, "Come closer, don't be afraid."

KIRSTEN: *Were you afraid?*

MACK: No. I said all right and I came closer and then she said, "What's your name?" I said Mack. "Where do you live?" I said, here and then…

PEGEEN: What did she say?

MACK: She said to come back tomorrow at the same time and then the bubble popped and she was gone.

CORTEZ: This has gone far enough. If you don't stop these stories we're going to have to prosecute you for aggravating the public, inciting and deteriorating the public's idea of the hereafter.

KIRSTEN: *And the thereafter.*

CORTEZ: You are a liar and a fool. Are your parents telling you to say these things:
MACK: No.
CORTEZ: So they can make money?
MACK: No.
KIRSTEN: *Where are the parents?*
PEGEEN: Both dead.
PRODUCER: *Interesting*
KIRSTEN: *Maybe it's your imagination.*
MACK: No it's not. I don't have any imagination in fact I could never think up anything like this. It's impossible.
CORTEZ: This is turning into a carnival, a kinderfest. What church do you go to?
MACK: None.
CORTEZ: Are you Catholic? This sounds like the Catholics.
MACK: Not Catholic.
CORTEZ: What are you then?
MACK: Nothing.
CORTEZ: How can you be unaffiliated with a religion and think up all of this, someone must be feeding you all this.
MACK: No one is feeding.
CORTEZ: What religion are your parents?
MACK: No religion.
PEGEEN: Have you read the Bible?
MACK: No Bible.
CORTEZ: You've been quoting from the Bible. What religion is she?
PEGEEN: Who?

KIRSTEN. *Who?*

CORTEZ: The girl in the ball.

MACK: She didn't say she was anything.

CORTEZ: This is Catholic propaganda, a Jesuit plot. Who is the Pope?

MACK: What is the pope?

CORTEZ: Surely you know what the pope is.

MACK: What is the Pope?

CORTEZ: Are you Jewish?

MACK: No.

CORTEZ: Have you ever been in a church?

MACK: No.

CORTEZ: Call the bishop.

PRODUCER: *He's fishing m the Bahamas.*

CORTEZ: Then get his secretary.

PEGEEN: She's with him.

CORTEZ: Don't tell me that.

KIRSTEN: *But she is.*

CORTEZ: Then get a priest or an underling. This is a Catholic plot.

DOC: *They can't do anything.*

PRODUCER: *Don't get the Catholics involved.*

CORTEZ: Then call the Archbishop of Canterbury or a rabbi.

KIRSTEN: *Call the Buddha why don't ya?*

PRODUCER *Don't get him involved.*

CORTEZ: Do you know anything about the Bible?

MACK: No, sir.

CORTEZ: What was she wearing

MACK: Nothing

- 155 -

CORTEZ: Do you take drugs?

MACK: No.

CORTEZ: Why are you telling everyone about this.

MACK: I'm not.

CORTEZ: Then how did they find out? The people from the television and all?

MACK: They followed you.

CORTEZ: This is a cult. Do you think you'll make money from this?

MACK: No.

CORTEZ: How much did the people from the television pay you?

MACK: Nothing.

CORTEZ: How much did they pay you?

MACK: Nothing.

CORTEZ: Did they offer you money?

MACK: Yes.

CORTEZ: Did you take it?

MACK: No.

CORTEZ: Did you take it?

MACK: No.

CORTEZ: You took the money.

MACK: No I didn't.

CORTEZ: How much did they pay you?

MACK: Nothing.

CORTEZ: How much did they offer you?

MACK: A thousand.

CORTEZ: Why didn't you take it?

MACK: I didn't want it.

CORTEZ: Why did they give you the money?

MACK: They didn't give it to me.

CORTEZ: Why did they offer it to you then? Don't get smart with me.

MACK: They wanted me to take them to the place.

CORTEZ: They knew where the place was?

MACK: They wanted me to make her show up on the film, if they paid me. I wouldn't take it.

CORTEZ: And so did she show up on the film?

MACK: They stayed there all day and…

CORTEZ: Then what?

MACK: And they developed the film and it was all orange.

CORTEZ: Kodak?

MACK: No, just orange.

PEGEEN: What kind of orange? A bluish orange? A reddish orange?

MACK: Sort of a reddish orange.

PEGEEN: Sort of like this dress?

KIRSTEN: *It must have been a bad roll.*

CORTEZ: Did they try again?

MACK: Yes. Then they offered me five thousand and I said no and they came anyway and the film came out but she wasn't on it.

CORTEZ: She was there. The camera never lies.

MACK: The camera didn't pick it up.

CORTEZ: But I saw some film with a woman standing there.

MACK: That was a fake, she doesn't look like that.

CORTEZ: She looks exactly like you said she looks.

MACK: But that wasn't her it was an actress. She doesn't look like that. They got it all wrong.

CORTEZ: Who shot the film?

MACK: They did.

CORTEZ: Is it a fake? Is it?

KIRSTEN: *Certainly not. My crew shot it.*

CORTEZ: It's a fake.

KIRSTEN: *Are you accusing me of lying?*

CORTEZ: You are lying. It's a fake.

KIRSTEN: *I was there and shot the film.*

CORTEZ: Did you see her?

KIRSTEN: *No.*

CORTEZ: Then how did you know where to point the camera?

KIRSTEN: *We pointed in the direction that she was talking* in and it developed with this woman on it.

CORTEZ: Who is an actress. So you believe him now. All I'm saying is that I don't believe his story about the woman in the basketball and if I don't believe that then how can I believe you shooting film of her? If I believe you, then I have to believe him. Do you believe him?

PEGEEN: I didn't.

CORTEZ: And now you do?

KIRSTEN: *Yes I do.*

PEGEEN: The woman was there. She's on the film.

CORTEZ: So we have proof now of the woman in the basketball.

KIRSTEN: *I believe that he may have seen someone.*

CORTEZ: I don't believe he saw anyone but I believe that you hired an actress and put her up there in front of the film to make this all sound true.

PRODUCER: *We don't do that.*

CORTEZ: You'll do anything you can get your hands on. I want that film taken into custody.

KIRSTEN: *Take it.*

CORTEZ: I want the original negative.

KIRSTEN: *Go ahead, we can shoot another roll.*

CORTEZ: Oh, you mean the actress isn't out of town? Do you take drugs?

PEGEEN: No.

CORTEZ: Do vou take drugs?

MACK: No.

CORTEZ: Do you take drugs?

KIRSTEN: *No.*

CORTEZ: How do you feel about that?

MACK: Nothing.

CORTEZ: You should feel strongly on either side no matter what you feel on whatever side but you must feel strongly.

MACK: But why do you have to feel strongly?

CORTEZ: Don't you have an opinion on anything? How do you feel about this?

MACK: The woman on the film is not the woman I saw.
CORTEZ: So you're saying they're lying.
MACK: I wouldn't put it like that.
CORTEZ: How would you put it?
MACK: There may have been some other woman there when they shot it.
CORTEZ: But you were there and you didn't see her.
MACK: I didn't see that one.
CORTEZ: Maybe they're twins.
MACK: Or they could be lying. But I would never call anyone a liar.
CORTEZ: Why not?
MACK: To call anyone a liar is vanity and a chase after the wind.
CORTEZ: Very good. Who told you that?
MACK: No one.
CORTEZ: Did the woman tell you this?
MACK: No.
CORTEZ: I'm going to get to the bottom of this.
PEGEEN: You are at the bottom of this.
CORTEZ: Shut him up.
MACK: Vanity, vanity of toil without profit.
CORTEZ: What are you saying?
MACK: Therefore I loathed life since for me the work that is done under the sun is evil for all is vanity and a chase after the wind.
PEGEEN: You never said that before.
MACK: Nothing.

PEGEEN: He's beginning to sound like a fortune cookie.

CORTEZ: Are you Catholic?

MACK: No.

CORTEZ: What does that mean?

MACK: What does what mean?

CORTEZ: Chase after the wind.

MACK: You know, futility, like an attempt to corral the winds, an infliction of the spirit.

PEGEEN: Can we stop this now?

CORTEZ: Now we are not going to stop this till we get to the bottom of this.

(*MACK resumes singing loudly until KIRSTEN interrupts.*)

KIRSTEN: But we are at the bottom.

PEGEEN: I'll stay here as long as you will.

CORTEZ: Are you threatening me? I'll have you arrested and put in a birdbath.

PRODUCER: Our conversation has deteriorated.

KIRSTEN: Oh, yes indeed.

CORTEZ: Don't speak until you are spoken to. Do you hear me?

MACK: Yes.

CORTEZ: Now, the second vision.

MACK: That was the second vision.

CORTEZ: How many have you had?

MACK: Thirteen.

CORTEZ: And when will the next one be?

(Cut)

(CORTEZ in chair. Day shot of window on monitors.)

KIRSTEN: So?

CORTEZ: I saw something last night.

KIRSTEN: You saw nothing last night.

CORTEZ: I saw something last night. Do you hear me?

KIRSTEN: I don't hear you. You saw nothing last night and that's that. Period.

CORTEZ: No period. I saw something last night whether it was there or not, it was there. It wasn't there but I saw it.

KIRSTEN: You saw nothing at all.

CORTEZ: I saw something.

KIRSTEN: You will tell no one about this.

CORTEZ: Until I see it again, I will tell nobody but you.

KIRSTEN: Don't tell me, I won't be listening.

CORTEZ: You will listen and I will see it again.

KIRSTEN: You don't want to see it again because you never saw it.

CORTEZ: I want to see it again and I will see it. Whatever it is.

KIRSTEN: Whatever it isn't, you won't see it ever again. That was the last time you will ever see it. You saw it once and forever and never again. Do you understand me?

CORTEZ: No, I don't understand you.

KIRSTEN: Please don't see it again.

CORTEZ: I can't help it. I saw it.

(Cut)

(CORTEZ on diagonally opposite monitors.
KIRSTEN paces from one to the other.)

CORTEZ: *Right.*
KIRSTEN: Wrong.
CORTEZ: *Right. I will see it again.*
KIRSTEN: You're not supposed to see it and
you won't.
CORTEZ: *I will see it again then just because of*
that.
KIRSTEN: You fool.
CORTEZ: *Agnus dei qui tollis pecata mundi*
miserere nobis.
KIRSTEN: Shut up.
CORTEZ: *Agnus dei.*
KIRSTEN: Why are you talking like that?
CORTEZ: *Blaspheming against the Lord. It told me*
to say that, he taught me and I taught you that and
now you're spitting it back to me out of context, out
of order, out of the wild blue yonder and you will...
KIRSTEN: Shut up immediately.
CORTEZ: *Agnus dei.*
KIRSTEN: Not one scintilla of a word out of
you now get out. I cannot bear the thought of
you.
CORTEZ: *Woe to you my foolish shepherd who*
forsakes his flock. May the sword fall upon his arm
and upon his right eye. Let his arm wither away
entirely and his right eye be blind forever. Open
your doors O Lebanon that the fire may devour
your cedars. Wail you cypress trees for the tears

have fallen, the mighty have been despoiled, wail you oaks of Bashan for the impenetrable forest is cut down. Hark, the wailing of the shepherds. Their glory has been ruined. Hark, the roaring of the young lions, the jungle of the Jordan is laid waste.
KIRSTEN: And I don't have to sit here while you pontificate endlessly to the wind. So don't.
CORTEZ: *I won't.*
KIRSTEN: Windwag. Endless pontification endlessly. An endless sermon on the mount. Beat it.
CORTEZ: *I am the pie in the sky, the center of the lie, the fool on the hill, the pill in the swill, the widows' watch, the eye of the needle, the slide rule, the key, the alpha, the omega, the Betamax, the blind mind, the morning noon and night. Do you understand me?*
KIRSTEN: Yes, I understand you completely.
CORTEZ: *Don't tell me that.*
KIRSTEN: Why not?
CORTEZ. *But above all, the frog prince, the ultra twister, jack the wack, the boogie man, the midnight special.* KIRSTEN: *Goodnight dear.*
(Cut)

MACK seated at small table, CORTEZ standing PEGEEN: seated at large table, gets up to read report. On interior monitor, KIRSTEN holds glass of water up to her face and inspects it. On ambient monitors, wind-blown trees.

KIRSTEN: *Oh dear, it's rained.*

PEGEEN: All over everything.

PRODUCER: *Now is it true that she appears near water?*

CORTEZ: Maybe near this glass of water.

MACK: Maybe.

CORTEZ: This glass of water is supposedly alleged to be from the stream that gushed forth. What if I spilled it.

PRODUCER: *Spill it.*

KIRSTEN: *What would happen?*

MACK: Nothing. I don't know. Just don't spill it.

CORTEZ: The water in itself doesn't represent anything?

MACK: No.

CORTEZ: So why couldn't I spill it?

MACK: You could.

KIRSTEN. Okay.

CORTEZ: It wouldn't hurt anything if I did would it?

MACK: No.

DOC: *What if 1 drank it?*

MACK: Then it would hurt you.

DOC. *Why?*

MACK: Because it would. You're not supposed to drink it.

PEGEEN: What's in it?

KIRSTEN: *Just water particles.*

PRODUCER: *Let's see the scientific report.*

PEGEEN: Now one pharmacist tested the water and found it disgusting in content as if a sewer pipe had exploded. But then a chemist from the NPN analyzed it and found, let me read- "that it contained some primary elements in superabundance: chlorides, carbonates, silicates, iron oxides, soda sulphates, etc. etc., very easily digested and imparting to the bodily system a disposition favorable to the balance of vital functioning. Its constituent substances lead them to believe it is a mineral spring. But that was contradicted by another scientist who in his analysis says it has led him to regard the water in question as a drinking water containing the same elements as most of the spring water met with in the mountains and more particularly those whose soil is rich in limestone, so that he says it is not a mineral spring but an ordinary spring."
CORTEZ: And so what? So what?
PRODUCER: *And what can you make of all that information?*
KIRSTEN: *Now you say she told you to dig for this well and drink from it'*
MACK: Yes.
PRODUCER: *How far down was it?*
MACK: You know all this.
KIRSTEN: *How far down was it?*
MACK: I dug down a foot or so and it started oozing up.

CORTEZ: Now isn't this where you stuck your face in the mud and the crowd laughed?
MACK: Yes
CORTEZ: Why would she tell you to stick your face in the mud?
MACK: She didn't.
CORTEZ: But you did.
MACK: I had to drink the water somehow.
DOC: *What did it taste like?*
MACK: When it first came up it was muddy but then it got clear and it was fine.
PRODUCER: *What are the doctor's findings?*
DOC: *After more than a few CAT scans I have found…(He reads from a report.) "Mack is of a delicate constitution, with a lymphatic and nervous temperament Thirteen years old though he seems not more than eleven His face is pleasant, his eyes have a lively expression. His head is regular in shape but narrow and rather on the small side His health he states is very good He has never suffered from headaches, has experienced no nervous attacks, he eats, drinks and sleeps wonderfully well. However, young Mack doesn't have the good health one might imagine He is obviously afflicted with asthma His breathing is slightly irregular and wheezing and at times becomes perceptibly so."*
CORTEZ: Why does he appear then to throw himself on the ground and bite the earth in his attacks of delirium?
PRODUCER- *I have never seen one of these attacks of delirium.*

PEGEEN: Are you trying to fasten the blame indirectly?

CORTEZ: Doesn't he or does he not bite the dust or sand when he is in a state of hallucination?

PRODUCER: *Exaltation.*

DOC: *There is nothing to prove that Mack has had any intention of imposing upon the public. This child is of an impressionable nature. He has possibly been the victim of an hallucination No doubt a reflection from the light of the water he so usually frequents caught his attention His imagination is influenced by a mental predisposition and caused him to imagine…*

CORTEZ: As many children do a figure resembling a statue in a church or book or painting.

KIRSTEN: *He's never been in a church.*

CORTEZ: He relates this vision to his friends and they drag him off to the beach.

KIRSTEN: *They follow him.*

CORTEZ: The rumor spreads around town and everyone starts screaming miracle and apparition. Several religions try to claim or reject him.

PRODUCER: *This is a medical report. Let's stick to medicine.*

DOC: *Surely the child's would-be young mind would naturally be more and more affected by this and his exaltation would work up into a peak, wound up tight like a spring.*

KIRSTEN: *Twister.*
CORTEZ: Tornado.
DOC: *Exactly, so what first was a mere hallucination gains more and more control over his mind, it begins to absorb him and isolate him from the outside real world And at the moment the hallucination becomes an apparition, at that point it results in a genuine state of ecstasy, a mental lesion…*
CORTEZ: That places the one affected by it under the domination of the absorbing idea.
DOC: *Consequently, the undersigned consider that the boy Mack may possibly have exhibited a state of ecstasy that has recurred several times. There is here a case of mental disease the effects of which explain the phenomena of the vision.*
CORTEZ: So we admit that it is an hallucination, an ecstasy resulting from a cerebral lesion. That is possible, very possible. It is even very probable. I myself follow this method of reasoning in practice.
DOC: *I merely observe that I believe in the possibility of the supernatural but I await further proofs before seeing it in the present case*
KIRSTEN: *If they're not from the Bible they must be from somewhere?*
PEGEEN: Oh, who cares?
KIRSTEN: *Would you like a roast-beef sandwich?*
MACK: No.
PRODUCER: *Don't be cruel.*
PEGEEN: Milk and honey?

MACK: I hate milk. I don't drink milk.

KIRSTEN: Water?

MACK: Yes.

PEGEEN: You've been drinking water for a month.

MACK: So what.

KIRSTEN: Don't you, aren't you hungry for anything else?

MACK: No.

PEGEEN: You're going to starve.

MACK: Do I look like I'm starving?

KIRSTEN: No.

MACK: Didn't the doctors test me and tell you that I was healthy?

PEGEEN: Yes.

MACK: Then why do I have to eat roast-beef sandwich or milk or honey or anything else but water? If I don't need anything but water then who needs anything else?

KIRSTEN: What's in that water?

MACK: Drink it and find out.

KIRSTEN: What's in it?

PEGEEN: Didn't the doctors test it and tell you what was in it?

PRODUCER: Yes

MACK: So that's what I'm living on.

KIRSTEN: It's just water particles in it. Just water in it.

MACK: So that's what it is. Why don't you drink it?

PEGEEN: You wouldn't let us.

KIRSTEN: *And everyone's afraid to drink it.*
PRODUCER: *They won't even look at it.*
MACK: Drink it.
KIRSTEN: *No, I don't want to.*
MACK: Go on.
PEGEEN: No, I won't.
MACK: Drink it I said
KIRSTEN: *Mack.*
MACK: I said drink it, I said.
PEGEEN: I will not drink it.
MACK: You will drink it.
PEGEEN: No.
MACK: I said drink it I said and I said drink it
and you will drink it because I said drink it.
KIRSTEN: *I will not drink it.*
 MACK: I'll ask you one more time.
PEGEEN: I'm not going to drink it.
MACK: Don't spill it.
KIRSTEN: *I'm going to spill it*
MACK: Drink it. Just a sip.
PEGEEN: (Takes a sip and spits it out.) It's
disgusting. Putrefied.

(Cut)

*(MACK still at small table, KIRSTEN standing in
front of chair opposite. CORTEZ standing at one
end of large table facing MACK. Day window on
all monitors.)*

MACK: Now taste it, the sanctity, the holiness. It's the way of the world.

KIRSTEN: How would you know about the way of the world? All I taste is dirt, mud- ugh.

MACK: Keep chewing, don't spit it out. Don't reject the holy consequence.

KIRSTEN: Forget the consequence, I'm spitting.

MACK: Don't.

KIRSTEN: Sorry.

CORTEZ: How could you do that?

KIRSTEN: I'm sorry it just tastes like dirt to me. What do you taste?

CORTEZ: Nothing really. It sort of tastes like chocolate. Chocolate.

KIRSTEN: It's dirt.

CORTEZ: It tastes like dirt. It is dirt.

MACK: Taste it again.

KIRSTEN: What are you trying to make us do?

MACK: Taste it again.

KIRSTEN: Please.

MACK: Taste it again I said.

KIRSTEN: Forget it. It tastes like dirt.

MACK: It is dirt. It's the dirt of the Lord. From heaven. Heavenly dirt.

KIRSTEN: What's it supposed to do? Cure us? Heavens to betsy.

MACK: Sort of in a way.

CORTEZ: Sort of in a way what?

KIRSTEN: Sort of or not sort of?

CORTEZ: This is not dirt it's chocolate.

KIRSTEN: You're telling us to eat chocolate and telling us it's dirt?

CORTEZ: This is chocolate.

MACK: It's dirt. Just plain dirt from the spring.

KIRSTEN: So why eat it then?

MACK: It doesn't matter how it tastes, it's that it's good for you.

CORTEZ: Like medicine.

MACK: I told you I don't believe in medicine.

CORTEZ: It's holy dirt from the holy spring.

MACK: Do you feel it diffusing through your body?

KIRSTEN: No I don't.

MACK: Strengthening you?

KIRSTEN: I do not feel a thing.

CORTEZ: This is chocolate.

KIRSTEN: What's it supposed to taste like?

MACK: Like dirt because it is dirt and if it's dirt it tastes like dirt and if you taste chocolate then that's what you taste.

CORTEZ: I'm tired of your alchemical, metaphysical tricks. Trickery, blasphemy, heresy and collusion with the devil and dirt farmers.

KIRSTEN: Dirt from the holy wellspring.

CORTEZ: That's not a holy well.

MACK: Spring.

CORTEZ: That's not a holy well.

MACK: Spring.

CORTEZ: It's not a holy spring.

KIRSTEN: There's nothing holy about it except that it's a hole.

CORTEZ: It's not a holy well.

KIRSTEN: First he gets us to drink that muddy water and now we're eating that holy hell springwellwater.

CORTEZ: Chocolate water.

KIRSTEN: If nothing else it's chocolate I know it.

MACK: It is not chocolate. It's dirt. Holy dirt from the holy spring.

CORTEZ: Dirty well water.

KIRSTEN: What's in that bag?

MACK: Nothing.

KIRSTEN: What's in that bag?

CORTEZ: There's a dead bird in it.

KIRSTEN: What's that doing in there?

MACK: I was going to feed the bird the dirt.

KIRSTEN: And cure it?

MACK: Yes.

CORTEZ: Well go ahead.

MACK: No, no. It's wrecked. You've wrecked the holiness. You know you're making me really mad saying this is chocolate.

KIRSTEN: Get that bird out of here and throw this mud out.

CORTEZ: It's chocolate, chocolate, chocolate!

MACK: Oh, wherefore art thou God? You're trying to make a fool out of me. Turning this all around and making a joke out of it.

KIRSTEN: How do you expect not to be a fool when you make people eat dirt.

MACK: It's not dirt.

CORTEZ: Chocolate! You're turning this all around and making it silly. It's holy. Holy dirt or chocolate, I think it's gone far enough. And they took the body out of the reliquary and plundered it all over the church floor, scattered it, created a sacrilege out of it.

KIRSTEN: Stop it. You're getting hysterical. Stop.

CORTEZ: And when they had created a sacrilege the skies poured down an apocalypse. They threw the toe over here and the teeth over there and paraded the head down the main street of Potsdam for everyone to see that the incorruptible body would in fact be corrupted and could not indeed fight back. How could it fight back when its fists were in separate parts of the world? When its clavicle was in the Philippines and its ear was in Italy and its toe was in Potsdam. How could they expect it to fight back.What could the poor dried-up remnants do?

KIRSTEN: Stop it. Now honey, sit down.

CORTEZ: Don't call me honey.

KIRSTEN: Now, now, now, now, now, honey calm down.

CORTEZ: I will not calm down.

KIRSTEN: No, no, no, no, no, no, no, no. Now listen to us.

CORTEZ: Oh, yes, yes, yes, yes, yes, yes, yes, yes.

KIRSTEN: Don't call me honey.

MACK: Now, honey, now.

KIRSTEN: Clam up.

(Cut)

(PEGEEN: and MACK in chairs. DOC at small table. On monitors, shot of old docks, pilings and water.)

CORTEZ: I was cooking one day and I was cooking a vegetable soup from scratch and I noticed there were little bits of meat floating around in the soup and I knew I hadn't put meat into the soup because I don't eat meat and there was no meat in the house anyway.

PEGEEN: And what did you do?

CORTEZ: Well, I threw the soup out onto the lawn in back of my house and the lawn caught fire. So I went to put it out and it wouldn't go out soI threw everything I could on it and it still wouldn't go out. Then I went and threw holy water on it and it blazed even higher. By this time the neighbors had started to notice what was happening and tried to help. Then it caught onto the house and we called the fire department and they took so long to get there and the house became a flaming disaster. It was just glowing and it was glowing so big and we couldn't figure out why because there wasn't much in the house to make it glow up so big and the

*firemen just couldn't get it out. The more water
they put on the more it would glow and the higher
it would get. There was just nothing to demolish a
fire of such magnitude. So we started praying or I
started praying and everyone prayed with me and
slowly the fire started to stop glowing so much and
suddenly it went right out just like a light bulb, just
right out. It was light and bright and suddenly it
got dark and was out and there was just a bit of
smoke wiping around. We were all shocked of
course and then we noticed that the residue of the
fire was this weird white residue.*

PEGEEN: And then what happened?

*CORTEZ: Not much. I stayed at a friend's house
and we swept up the residue into big piles. There
was nothing left of the house, just a big square of
residue. 1 had cut my hand on something the week
before and after I had finished sweeping up the ash 1
looked at my hand and there was no cut on it
anymore, blow the hand remembered that there had
been a cut on it too. But there was no cut anywhere,
not even on the other hand so it was a miracle.*

PEGEEN: Hardly.

CORTEZ: Why not?

PEGEEN: There are all sorts of explanations for
things like that.

CORTEZ: Like what?

PEGEEN: Who put the meat in the soup?

CORTEZ: It was the devil.

PEGEEN: How do you know that?

CORTEZ: Because I don't eat meat.

PEGEEN: Let's skip to the next incident.

CORTEZ: *Is it true that the week after you were found…*

PEGEEN:…biting the walls of your parish church?

CORTEZ: *Oh yes.*

PEGEEN: Have you had these fits before?

CORTEZ: *No. The doctors said it was a cerebral malfunction.*

PEGEEN: Who made you bite the walls?

CORTEZ: *It think it was God.*

MACK: I see. And why did you bite the walls?

CORTEZ:*I hated them.*

PEGEEN: You hated the walls so you bit them.

CORTEZ: *Please don't laugh, it's not funny.*

PEGEEN: 1 think it is.

CORTEZ: *Why?*

PEGEEN: Because it is silly. Were you diabolically possessed?

CORTEZ: *No.*

PEGEEN: Why did you bite the walls?

CORTEZ: *Was this the first time you bit the church wall? Yes.*

PEGEEN: Was this the first time you bit a wall of any kind?

CORTEZ: *Yes.*

PEGEEN: How long after the fire was this?

CORTEZ: *The next week.*

PEGEEN: And you say it was the god that made you do this.

CORTEZ: *Yes.*

PEGEEN: Which god?

CORTEZ: *The only one there is.*

PEGEEN: Which one is that?

CORTEZ: *I'm not here to answer that.*

PEGEEN: How did you say your house blew up.

CORTEZ: *I didn't say it blew up, it burned.*

PEGEEN: You said it blew up. I have it recorded in the interview that you said your house blew up.

CORTEZ: *I never said that.*

PEGEEN: It's here. Shall we play it back? How did you say your house blew up? How did you say your house blew up?

CORTEZ: *Well, it was the fire that caught from the lawn and it caught onto the house.*

PEGEEN: I see. And why did this happen?

CORTEZ: *The pot of stew was possessed by the devil meat and it caught the lawn on fire when I threw it out the window. And it was some kind of miracle and then I saw the lady over by the water. The house just blew up and burned miraculously.*

PEGEEN: It was a gas leak.

CORTEZ: *It was a miracle.*

PEGEEN: It was a gas leak, the authorities have studied it and it was a gas leak, nothing else.

CORTEZ: *How does it explain the meat in the pot? I never have meat in the house.*

PEGEEN: The only thing we can explain is the gas leak and explosion.

MACK: Thank you very much.

DOC: How could you do that to him?

PEGEEN: It's my job. I'm known as a nutcracker. I'm paid to make them un-believe what they believe. We just can't go around having houses explode for any reason. I'll admit it's an oddity but that's all I'll admit. I don't know who put the meat in the pit.

DOC: Pot.

PEGEEN: Pit, pot, pisspot. He's obviously a nut and I hate hallucinations. On to the next hallucination.

DOC: Exorcism.

PEGEEN: I don't exorcise. I disbelieve, dehallucinate, erase, expose. On to the next one. Can you hear me? Can you hear me? Yes? Good.

(Cut)

(Moving rollercoaster images on all video screens. MACK seated at large table, PEGEEN and CORTEZ pacing. Midway through scene, PEGEEN helps MACK into a white and gold toreador jacket.)

PEGEEN: Would you have any reason to, or are you being paid by the church?

CORTEZ: Why would I be paid by the church? Are you being paid by a church?

MACK: Why would I be paid by a church?

PEGEEN: You might be paid to discredit what he's seen.

CORTEZ: And you might be paid to find some meaning in what he's saying.

PEGEEN: They need as many meanings as they can get.

CORTEZ: Maybe we're both being paid by as many churches as can pay us on either side.

PEGEEN: Why would churches want to get involved in all these exploding houses and so on?

CORTEZ: The cures.

PEGEEN: They want as many as they can get.

MACK: Proved.

PEGEEN: Proved or unproved.

CORTEZ: Bully for you.

PEGEEN: Bully for me.

CORTEZ: So if we both agree that we're both being paid.

PEGEEN: But we're not. Neither of us.

CORTEZ: Don't jump down my neck.

PEGEEN: Get your foot off my throat.

CORTEZ: And 1 won't jump on your neck.

PEGEEN: What do you think about all of this?

CORTEZ: Do you think we're being paid by a church?

PEGEEN: Any church?

MACK: Would they pay you?

CORTEZ: I don't think so.

MACK: Have they offered to?

PEGEEN: No.

MACK: Are you lying?

CORTEZ: No.

MACK: Which one of you is being paid?

PEGEEN: Neither of us.

MACK: What about her?

PEGEEN: I'm not.

MACK: And him?

CORTEZ: No.

PEGEEN: So none of us are being paid by any church any old church from nowhere so let's go on. How did the dog die?

CORTEZ: Which dog?

PEGEEN: The dog that was cured. That was the first cure was it not?

CORTEZ: Yes, that we know of.

PEGEEN: Let him answer.

MACK: Yes.

PEGEEN: It was hit by a car and died and was buried by its owners and they de-buried it and unearthed it.

CORTEZ: Exhumed it.

MACK: Thank you and brought it to the spring and stuck its head in it and they left it there soaking for...

CORTEZ: How long?

MACK: Half an hour.

PEGEEN: More or less?

MACK: Less. And then we were sitting there watching it and suddenly it let out this huge groan and started breathing and got up again and started drinking the water and jumping and running around for joy.

PEGEEN: Do you think it was happy that it was alive? CORTEZ: Of course it was, it didn't want to be dead.

MACK: And then they took it back to the doctor and there was nothing wrong with it.

CORTEZ: What was wrong with it when it died?

MACK: Its body was all smashed up and strangled by the car that hit it. There was no way it could have survived that car.

PEGEEN: And the people that hit it were so happy The doctor's report says that it was dead on arrival Suffering multiple contusions and lacerations to all parts of the body and brain as well as internal injuries and broken hipbone, collar bone, arms and legs fractured multiple to the head- skull.

MACK: And it was dead and buried.

CORTEZ: How long was it buried before they…

PEGEEN: Unearthed…

CORTEZ: Exhumed it.

MACK: A week.

PEGEEN: Was there any sign of mortality on the body?

MACK: Meaning what?

PEGEEN: Meaning any decomposition of the flesh Any sign of parasitical insects or organisms invading the corpse.

MACK: None whatsoever.

CORTEZ: Any odor extracting out of it?

PEGEEN: No in fact the owners said that a wonderful flowery odor accompanied the corpse of the body.

CORTEZ: Like what smell?

MACK: Like a flowery smell. Perfumy.

CORTEZ: There wasn't any embalming applied to the animal MACK: None whatsoever.

CORTEZ: And what do the owners think what happened? MACK: They think it's a miracle.

 CORTEZ: What religion are they?

MACK: None.

CORTEZ: What religion were they as children?

PEGEEN: They're listed as atheistic.

CORTEZ: Do they attend church now?

MACK: What for?

CORTEZ: In thanks.

MACK: No they don't

PEGEEN: Have they changed their atheistic lifestyle because of this incident?

MACK: Not at all.

CORTEZ: They must have changed in some way. 'Your dog doesn't come back to life and you just stay the same PEGEEN:Why not?

CORTEZ: It just doesn't happen that way.

PEGEEN: It has happened that way. They're just thankful and accept it and are happy.
CORTEZ: Thankful to who?
PEGEEN: Not to anyone.
MACK: To the dog.
CORTEZ: Why to the dog?
MACK: For coming back.
PEGEEN: Has the dog changed?
CORTEZ: Except for the fact that it came back to life, nothing has changed.
MACK: He eats the same.
PEGEEN: Eats the same, everything the same. Still answers to the same name?
CORTEZ: Does he drink the holy water?
MACK: Won't go near it.
PEGEEN: Why not?
MACK: Will not drink it since that first day. Won't go near it.
PEGEEN: They can lead a dog to water but they can't make him drink it.
MACK: He just turns away.
CORTEZ: Let's just drop it for now it's a dead end.
PEGEEN: Hardly a dead end.
CORTEZ: It doesn't prove anything. They could all be lying.
PEGEEN: Why would you say that?
CORTEZ: You saw the dead dog.
MACK: It looked dead, I don't know if it was dead.
PEGEEN: Was there blood all over it?

CORTEZ: Yes, but it could have been paint and the dog could have been on a drug.

PEGEEN: But there's a doctor's report.

CORTEZ: It could have been faked.

PEGEEN: Everyone has sworn to the facts about the dead dog. Do you believe it came back to life?

MACK: Yes.

PEGEEN: So you don't think it was paint or drugs that made the dog look dead?

MACK: No.

PEGEEN: So dead is dead.

MACK: Dead was dead.

PEGEEN: And nothing was faked. Nothing was faked, dead was dead and live is alive.

CORTEZ: That dog could have been faked.

MACK: It was in smithereens I told you!

PEGEEN: Everyone admits it was in smithereens.

CORTEZ: All right, it was in smithereens.

PEGEEN: And came back together.

CORTEZ: And it was not psychically improvised?

PEGEEN: It was not improvised.

CORTEZ: Psychically?

PEGEEN: By the dog or the owners or the boy so we can all agree to that.

CORTEZ: I can't agree on anything yet except the dog might have died and might have survived.

PEGEEN: Where is the dog?

CORTEZ: Now what about the reports that the dog spoke?

MACK: The dog never talked.

CORTEZ: I have reports that it spoke.

PEGEEN: What did it say?

MACK:I was there It didn't say anything.

CORTEZ: I told you it didn't say nothing.

PEGEEN: What did it say?

CORTEZ: Where is the dog?

PEGEEN: There it is.

CORTEZ: Ask it a question.

MACK: That dog never said nothing and you know it. You're just making this up.

CORTEZ: Well, it's among the investigative reports that I have.

PEGEEN: Who made them?

CORTEZ: Several veterinarians.

PEGEEN: Oh and on and on, who cares about the dog?

CORTEZ: Because it was the first instance of the cures.

PEGEEN: Why don't you talk to someone who was cured?

CORTEZ: You know that's impossible and that's just why you're asking me. All right. We all know it's impossible because of the fact that all the cured for some reason cannot speak.

PEGEEN: But they can write and they can…

CORTEZ: Now what about the reports that the doll spoke?

MACK: The doll never talked.

CORTEZ: I have reports that it spoke.

PEGEEN: What did it say?

MACK: I was there. It didn't say anything.

CORTEZ: To you it didn't say nothing.

PEGEEN: What did it say?

CORTEZ: Where is the doll?

PEGEEN: There it is.

CORTEZ: Ask it a question.

MACK: That doll never said nothing and you know it. You're just making this up.

CORTEZ: Well, it's among the investigative reports that I have.

PEGEEN: Who made them?

CORTEZ: Several veterinarians.

PEGEEN: Oh and on and on, who cares about the doll?

CORTEZ: Because it was the first instance of the cures.

PEGEEN: Why don't you talk to someone who was cured?

CORTEZ: You know that's impossible and that's just why you're asking me. All right, we all know it's impossible because of the fact that all the cured for some reason cannot speak.

PEGEEN: But they can write and they can…

(Cut)

(KIRSTEN paces back and forth. Ambient monitors show cars going by on a highway.)

CORTEZ: I don't even know what I've said.

KIRSTEN: You haven't said much.

CORTEZ: *Read it back to me.*

KIRSTEN: You wouldn't want to hear it, you're hysterical.

CORTEZ: *Even now?*

KIRSTEN: Even now, you're hysterical, not sparkling, flat and dull Your head is not a wonderful place to be in.

CORTEZ: *Oh, I know.*

KIRSTEN: Go home

CORTEZ: *And why aren't you a nut?*

KIRSTEN: Because I'm simply not.

CORTEZ: *Watch out for the car Why aren't you a nut?*

KIRSTEN: Because I'm simply and clearly not, but why?

CORTEZ: *Because I will vomit the truth Hear me out.*

KIRSTEN: Not on the rug. Not on the rug I said. Don't vomit the truth on my clean rug again, please don't do it.

CORTEZ: *We've had a lot of conversations.*

KIRSTEN: Sweaty conversations

CORTEZ: *On how to open our heads up from the top and let the truth vomit out.*

KIRSTEN: In.

CORTEZ: *Is it unconnectable?1 wanted it to become so clear It seemed so clear At critical moments it becomes so clear and now it's just become so unclear. The confusion was so clear m my mind I don't know how it was clear but it was at*

- 189 -

those few moments. And now that I'm being clearer there is no way to tell you in a clear way I'm just a nut going on and on. But why isn't he a nut? Why doesn't he sound like a nut? Maybe I look like a nut. Do 1 look like a nut?

KIRSTEN: You have such a wonderful sense of desperation but we can't use it for our show, it's much too desperate. You understand. You're a fruitcake.

CORTEZ: Don't be cruel

KIRSTEN: You are a stark raving lunatic do you understand?1 just cannot interview you on my show it's just going to be impossible You just aren't making yourself understood properly in a clear way I would love to but it's going to be impossible.

CORTEZ: You must interview me. I must get the message out.

KIRSTEN: It would be ridiculous to interview live or prerecorded. You're just crazy. You're having hallucinations. You should see a doctor.

CORTEZ: How can you say that about me?1 have this message that must go out to the world. You have to believe me.

KIRSTEN: Don't you understand? You're hysterical You're a hysteric. You're disrupting even yourself. You don't even know what you're talking about. You're babbling all kinds of idiotic evidence to the contrary of your own mouth.

CORTEZ: *You've got to believe me.*

KIRSTEN: You're hysterical.

CORTEZ: *But I'm not.*

KIRSTEN: I'm not going to argue this with you.

CORTEZ: *But we must at least argue. I have to get this message across.*

KIRSTEN: Your message is a mess

CORTEZ: *But we'll all burn.*

KIRSTEN: Then we will burn but you must see a doctor

CORTEZ: *God will turn his back on you.*

KIRSTEN: Have some water. Now, what is it you have to tell us.

CORTEZ: *I have been instructed.*

KIRSTEN: By who?

CORTEZ: *By her.*

KIRSTEN: To tell you...

CORTEZ: *That you have been frequently guilty of misrepresenting the truth and you must not misinterpret the message she gives to me to give to you.*

KIRSTEN: Okay. Now what is the message?

CORTEZ: *Please pray with me.*

PRODUCER: *Shut him up and get him out of here.*

KIRSTEN: We can't just throw him out.

PRODUCER: *Call in the cops.*

KIRSTEN: No, we can't call them. He'll make a scene.

PRODUCER: *I'm tired of hearing about blazing tuna and burned people. Somebody gimme a pigfoot!*

CORTEZ: *All of you must fall on your knees and play with me. And pray for us all.*
KIRSTEN: What do you think?
PRODUCER: *Wait till he collapses and then ship him back to where he came from.*
KIRSTEN: He'll come back. I'm going to read to you a transcription of what you told us last night and you tell me if it sounds like it makes sense to you.

(Cut)

(MACK on stool, KIRSTEN on monitor opposite.)

KIRSTEN: *Tell me the story again about the cure.*
MACK: *(His voice becomes more hysterical as he talks.)* I didn't have nothing to do with it. I was just standing there and I told them I had nothing to do with anything and I couldn't do anything and so not to come near me and they could go to the spring if they wanted to but they couldn't come near me. So I went home but they dragged me to the house and I could taste the poor mother's salt tears, they were all over my arms. Then he fell to the floor and cried a big long cry. Then someone picked him

up and his feet stuck out like they were dead. Shall I go to the hospital with you? No, I can go alone. They said I should go with you. No, I can go alone. I just want to get him right in there. I'll go with Pepito. I'll call Pepito. But I knew all about it. It was happening while I knew it was happening. I was scared, so I walked around the door and he was in there sleeping so I walked outside by the fence and someone was wailing. There was only one star out. Then, I walked by the door and they were in there and he was sleeping sick. I hear crying but I didn't believe it so 1 looked over by the bed and the mother cried and fell on me and I moved because I didn't want her tears to touch me. I don't want your hot sweaty salty tears to touch me. Then he picked his body up and the legs were stiff so I looked and cried and fell on the floor. My arm was out and my face was wet. Then I stood up and someone else was gone and they tried to push my hand on him and I said, "This is unchangeable, he's erased!" Then the body fell down and his back was to the floor forever. They pushed my hand on him but I didn't want to touch it! They wanted me to pray I said, "Get up, get up!" And he got up I screamed and ran away. Stop staring at me! What are you looking at?!

KIRSTEN: *I'll bet you did.*

MACK: They all ran after me.

(Cut)

(KIRSTEN seated at large table, MACK in a chair.)

PEGEEN: Shall we eat?

MACK: Of course.

KIRSTEN: What are we going to eat?

DOC: What time is it?

MACK: Five o'clock.

KIRSTEN: I thought it was four.

PEGEEN: It's four o'clock.

DOC: It's four isn't it? See my watch?

MACK: I said it's five and it's five, I said it.

KIRSTEN: Well…

MACK: I said it's five o'clock and let's eat.

DOC: All right.

MACK: What are we eating?

PEGEEN: Sandwiches.

MACK: I don't want sandwiches.

KIRSTEN: Why not?

MACK: I said I don't want sandwiches.

DOC: We'll have something else then

MACK: We certainly will. Where's the water?

KIRSTEN: What water?

MACK: I said I want the water now.

DOC: Oh.

MACK: Get the water I said. I said get the water. I said get the water didn't I?

PEGEEN: Yes.

MACK: Then get it and shut up.

PEGEEN: Shall we eat?

MACK: Of course.

KIRSTEN: What are we going to eat?

DOC: What time is it?

MACK: Five o'clock.

KIRSTEN: I thought it was four.

PEGEEN: It's four o'clock.

DOC: It's four isn't it? See my watch?

MACK: I said it's five and it's five. I said it.

KIRSTEN: Well.

MACK: I said it's five o'clock and let's eat.

DOC: All right.

MACK: What are we eating?

PEGEEN: Sandwiches.

MACK: I don't want sandwiches.

KIRSTEN: Why not?

MACK: I said I don't want sandwiches.

DOC: *We'll have something else then.*

MACK: We certainly will. Where's the water?

KIRSTEN: What water.

MACK: I said I want the water now.

DOC: *Oh.*

MACK: Get the water I said. I said get the
water. I said get the water didn't I?

PEGEEN: *Yes.*

MACK: Then get it and shut up.

(Cut)

KIRSTEN: and MACK: still seated.

MACK: This vale of tears.

PRODUCER: That poor withering priest.

MACK: And when I put my foot down, I put it down and when it stays down it stays down.
KIRSTEN: I don't know what you mean.
MACK: Shall we pray?
KIRSTEN: To who? To what?
PRODUCER: For what?
MACK: For you.
KIRSTEN: I never pray for myself.
PRODUCER: It's so fruitless.
KIRSTEN: So vain. Vanity, vanity, vanity of vanities. You are vanity. What profit a man from all the labor which he toils at under the sun. One generation passes and another comes but the world forever stays, right?
MACK: The sun rises and the sun goes down then it presses on to the place where it rises, blowing toward the south then toward the north. The wind turns again and again resuming its rounds. All rivers go to the sea yet never does the sea become full to the place where they go. The rivers keep on going. All speech is labored. There is nothing man can say. The eye is not satisfied with seeing nor is the ear filled with hearing. The sun rises and the sun goes down. Then it presses....
PRODUCER: *Oh, so what.*
KIRSTEN: Come on without, come on within.
PRODUCER: *You'll not see nothing like the Mighty* Quinn.
MACK: I cannot bear the thought of you.

KIRSTEN: The sun rises and the sun goes down.

MACK: Oh, shut up. Cast your bread on the waters after a long time you may find it again. Vanity, for all is vanity and a chase after the wind.

KIRSTEN: Idiot wind.

MACK: For as the crackling of thorns under a fire pot so is the fool's laughter This is also vanity. I saw her there floating up to the sky in a blue-green ball of nervousness.

KIRSTEN:And what else did you see?

MACK: A cloud. A purple cloud of miasma.

KIRSTEN:And what else?

MACK: A prison in the sky. She makes lightning flash in the rain and releases storm winds from their chambers, repeat that.

KIRSTEN: Every man is stupid, ignorant. Every artisan is put to shame by his idol. He has molded a fraud without breath of life. Nothingness. They are a ridiculous work. They will perish in their time of punishment. Right.

(Cut)

(DOC at small table, PEGEEN in chair opposite, MACK in chair. All video screens show KIRSTEN,PRODUCER, CORTEZ standing in front of car with headlights on.)

KIRSTEN: You've spent a month in silence.

DOC: You haven't said a word for a month.
PEGEEN: Say something.
PRODUCER Everyone is asking.
DOC: Please say something.
KIRSTEN: If you don't say something we'll have to say something for you.
PRODUCER: We're going to say something for you.
DOC: Speak.
PEGEEN: We're going to make up a statement for you.
KIRSTEN: They think we've trapped you in here and won't let you speak.
PRODUCER: Say something.
DOC: Have you seen anything?
PEGEEN: Did she come again?
PRODUCER: Have you seen anything? Anyone?
KIRSTEN: Have you seen any lights? Anything moving in the dark?
DOC: Heard anything?
PEGEEN: Any voices?
PRODUCER: Anyone say anything to you?
KIRSTEN: Had any dreams?
DOC: Have you decided anything?
PEGEEN: Is there anything we can do for you?
PRODUCER: Is there anything in the water?
KIRSTEN: There haven't been any cures for a month.
DOC: Is something wrong?
PEGEEN: Is she mad at you?

PRODUCER: Are you mad at her?

KIRSTEN: Does she appear anymore?

DOC: Is something wrong with the water?

PRODUCER: Speak.

PEGEEN: There are people waiting outside every day. Waiting for you.

KIRSTEN: There's a lot of sick people.

DOC: Everyone wants to know what's the matter with you.

PEGEEN: Say something.

PRODUCER: If he doesn't say something soon we're going to have to deny any connection or responsibility.

KIRSTEN: Say something.

DOC: Where is she? What happened to her?

PEGEEN: Is something wrong? How long are you going to sit there?

PRODUCER: Eat something at least.

KIRSTEN: It's been a month since you've eaten.

DOC: Eat something. Say something.

PEGEEN: Do you want some water?

PRODUCER: Say something.

MACK: No.

PEGEEN: What?

PRODUCER: No.

(Cut)

(DOC still at small table, KIRSTEN paces. MACK gets up, picks up glass of water and carries it around with him.)

KIRSTEN: Well then you have to locate her face, find me her face.
DOC: Why does this have to be so hard for you?
MACK: There's a fly in here. Kill it.
DOC: Why?
MACK: Kill it. Kill it.
DOC: Why?
MACK: I'm so scared of it. Kill it. What arrangements do you have for killing insects? They all must be removed from every room I enter. I cannot have insects around. This is a plot against me. Pick them out like sheep I said. I said it. Set them apart for the day of carnage. How long must the earth mourn and the green of the countryside wither. For even your own brothers, the members of your father's house betray you. They have recruited a force against you.
ALL: Do not believe them even if they are friendly to you in their words. Yet I like a trusting lamb led to the slaughter had not realized that they were hatching a plot against me.
MACK: Let us destroy the tree in its vigor. Let us cut him off from the land of the living so that his name will be spoken no more.
KIRSTEN: Enough.
DOC: Kinderfest.
KIRSTEN: But why?

MACK: They confuse me.

DOC: But how?

MACK: They're ugly. They confuse me and throw me off. They're tiny dead angels. Tiny Lucifers, flies on fire and so they must get out.

KIRSTEN: What are you digging for out there?

MACK: The spring, the water. It's under there.

DOC: How do you know?

KIRSTEN: Did she say something to you?

DOC: Did she come back?

MACK: No.

KIRSTEN: Why are you digging?

MACK: Because I know the spring is there. Get rid of these flies I said.

DOC: We're trying.

KIRSTEN: Why do they bother you so much?

MACK: Get rid of them I said.

DOC: All right.

MACK: I said get rid of them, didn't I?

KIRSTEN: Then get rid of them.

DOC: Okay.

MACK: I might breathe one in. Do you hear a breathing?

KIRSTEN: No.

DOC: It's nothing. A bird, a fly, a buzzard.

MACK: There is only one chair in this room. One room, one chair. We're going to burn in this house. A firefly will drift into the thatch and burn us right up. I'm a hootchie-coochie man, I'll get you one by one.

KIRSTEN: There's a fly out there. A bull ghost.

MACK: In the field out there. A bullfighter on a horn. He's stuck, he can't get off. What's in that glass there?

DOC: Scotch and ice.

MACK: Look in there. The whiskey is destroying the ice. Melting it away. Tearing it all away from itself. Is there a fly in here? I told you to get them out.

KIRSTEN: There aren't any flies in here, they're gone.

MACK: Then it's a mosquito.

KIRSTEN: What about all the people waiting outside. Don't you want to say something to them?

MACK: Let them eat rock underwater. I see a star up there and it's coming right down on all of us.

KIRSTEN: When?

MACK: Tonight.

KIRSTEN: Enough. You're either going to get up and say something to those people or we're calling an ambulance for intravenous feeding and I don't care what the hell anyone says.

MACK: Go ahead.

DOC: I will.

MACK: One house, one room, one chair, one ambulance, one doctor, one needle, one lady, one ball of fire, one cure, one fool, one fly, get it out.

KIRSTEN: This is your last chance, take it or leave it, because we're leaving it right now.

DOC: Are you going to perform a miracle?
MACK: No.
KIRSTEN: Are you going to see the lady again?
MACK: No.
DOC: Are you going to dig for water?
MACK: No.
KIRSTEN: Are you going to see the lady again?
MACK: No.
DOC: So no more miracle, no more water and no more lady.
MACK: In that order.
KIRSTEN: The ambulance is here, shall we go?
DOC: Sure.
KIRSTEN: What happened to the lady?
MACK: Nothing.
DOC: Where is she?
MACK: I said I don't want any flies in that car.
KIRSTEN: There won't be.
DOC: Intravenous.
MACK: Yes.
KIRSTEN: It's intravenous.
DOC: It'll be your anchor, it'll keep you from coming apart, it'll keep you docked in the harbor.
KIRSTEN: We're a pentangle, a triangle, invisible and indivisible, one nation under a groove. Get back into bed and shut up.
MACK: Hey, fuck you baby, don't order me around. This is my gig.
KIRSTEN: It was your gig and it's over.
MACK: You're trying to trip me up.

DOC: You've already tripped and fallen.

MACK: Then pick me up.

KIRSTEN: Pick yourself up and get into bed and shut up.

MACK: What do we do?

KIRSTEN: Lift your bundle and leave the land.

MACK: I will sling away the inhabitants of the land. I will hem them in that they may be undone, taken. Woe is me. I am undone. My wound is incurable yet I had thought if I make light of my wound, I can bear it. My tent is ruined.All its cords are severed. My sons have left me. They are no more. No one to pitch my tent. No one to raise its curtains. KIRSTEN:Yes. The shepherds were stupid as cattle. The Lord they sought not. Therefore they had no success. And all their flocks are scattered. Listen, a noise. It comes closer. A great uproar from the northern land to turn the cities of Judah into a desert haunt of jackals.

DOC: Jackasses.

KIRSTEN: Jackrabbits.

DOC: Jack shit.

ALL: Yeah all right!

MACK: Oh dear, dear me.

(Cut)

(DOC still at small table, KIRSTEN at large table, PRODUCER in chair.)

MACK: *Get this goon food out of here. Get it out I said. Silence!*

KIRSTEN: Silence.

DOC: But…

MACK: Silence I said.

KIRSTEN: Listen to the music.

MACK: Shall we pray?

DOC: All right.

MACK: Pray, sing.

KIRSTEN: And haven't you pretended to become some kind of religious fanatic?

DOC: Oh, and look at you poor thing. No one's said a thing about you. Never will.

KIRSTEN: Isn't it a fact that you were drunk on the beach the night you say you saw this vision? Some water

MACK: No

KIRSTEN: Some water.

MACK: No

DOC: And haven't you pretended all this time to be some kind of religious fanatic?

MACK: No.

KIRSTEN: And haven't you lied to everyone including your own lawyer and everyone else you've come into contact with? Isn't it true that you haven't told the truth since you said you saw this thing?

MACK: She's not a thing.

PRODUCER: And isn't it true that there isn't a thing or woman in a ball?

MACK: No

KIRSTEN: Isn't it true that there isn't a woman in a ball of light? There isn't a ball of light and that you've masterminded this whole thing? Manufactured this entire ping pong game to attract attention to yourself? And how much money have you made from all of this?

MACK: A dime!

KIRSTEN: You've made me pray to walls, to water. To anything you asked me to in search for an answer. You've made me learn prayers in Latin, Hebrew and anything else Songs, hymns, I don't know how many glasses of this holy water you've made me drink and all for nothing.

MACK: I didn't make you do anything.

DOC: Why are you so calm?

MACK: I'm calm because I'm right.

KIRSTEN: Wrong

(Cut)

(MACK stands facing a video monitor, on which is a river scene He clutches the sides of the monitor.) KIRSTEN is on the monitor behind him.)

KIRSTEN: *I want you to tell me everything calmly I want you to repeat everything you've said to me I want you to calmly tell me everything I want you to tell me everything calmly.*

MACK: I stole those eyes from the statue I didn't give them to any lady in a ball, I threw them into the river. Go and look for them. They're there. Do you think I gave jack shit if anyone was cured? No, I didn't I just talked and talked I never said there would be a cure but you thought there would be so there was I didn't do anything and so they all got cured I had nothing to do with it. Maybe there was a woman in a ball but I never saw her. She was never there when I was there. Maybe everyone else saw her but I sure didn't. But then I didn't like it anymore and there was no way to get out of it so I kept on telling it and then all these things started happening and happening and I couldn't stop them I even prayed to somebody to make them stop happening I even prayed to the lady in the ball to make them stop happening but she couldn't because she wasn't there I even tried to see her I tried and tried until my eyes got bloody I prayed every night for it all to stop and then it just kept happening. That's all I know, that's all there is to tell. Nothing ever happened to me. It just happened by itself. All I said was that I saw a woman in a ball and all these things started happening so fast. That's all I know That's all there is to tell. It was not a miracle. I don't even know why! What are you looking at?!

KIRSTEN: *Then what was it?*

MACK: It was luck. Pure fucking luck. I'm lucky. For worse or for better for better or for worse it was luck.

(Cut)

*(CORTEZ at small table. KIRSTEN, DOC, MACK
on monitors.)*
CORTEZ: There's one in here I can feel it Get it
out
KIRSTEN: There it is.
CORTEZ: Get out Get out
KIRSTEN: There it goes. It's gone.
CORTEZ: You diabolical little wretch.
MACK: I am aren't I?
CORTEZ: So.
KIRSTEN: What's the matter with you?
CORTEZ: I'm suffering from a diabolism. A
lesion of the mind, just like the doctor said.
KIRSTEN: All this stuff is just regurgitating out
of you.
CORTEZ: You are regurgitating out of me.
KIRSTEN: Where is it all coming from?
CORTEZ: My heart.
KIRSTEN: What heart?
CORTEZ: The black hole in my chest. Right
here. See it? That's where it's all coming out of.
MACK: And that's where the flies are coming
out of.
CORTEZ: Those flies are not coming out of me.
KIRSTEN: Yes, they are
MACK: We chased them away and they went
right back into you.
CORTEZ: Those flies are not coming out of me.

KIRSTEN: Yes, they are.

(Cut)

(DOC at small table, KIRSTEN and MACK standing. Monitors with night shot of glowing window. After "Atlantis," they switch to shot of brick wall.)

KIRSTEN: A thousand people are looking for you.
MACK: It's an oil well.
DOC: It looks like Buckwheat.
MACK: It looks like Buckwheat I said.
KIRSTEN: Now when this plane lands I want you to be polite to the reporters.
MACK: I hate them.
DOC: They're trying to help you. They're supporting your story.
MACK: I hate them and I want to kill them all.
KIRSTEN: But they're your friends.
MACK: No, they're not. They're trying to trip me up. Trip me up and make me fall over and I don't mean maybe.
KIRSTEN: Just stay cool and answer the questions.
MACK: Just answer the *questions (He lies on his back on large table.)*
KIRSTEN: I wrote the questions, you have to answer them and don't answer any questions I

didn't write. What's the answer to number four?

MACK: Separation of church and state.

KIRSTEN: Correct.

MACK: My eyes are burning. I want you to tell me everything calmly I want you to repeat everything you've said to me. I want you to calmly tell me everything. I want you to tell me everything calmly.

KIRSTEN: *(Washes MACK's eyes during the following speech.)*Try this one on for size. "There was an island which lay before the great flood in the area we now call the Atlantic Ocean. So great an area of land that from her western shores those beautiful sailors journeyed to the South and the North Americas with ease in their ships with painted sails. To the east, Africa was her neighbor across a short strait of sea miles." Go and look for them. They're there. Do you think I gave a shit if anyone was cured? No, I didn't. I just talked and talked. I never said there would be a cure but you thought there would be so there was. I didn't do anything and so they all got cured. I had nothing to do with it. *(Blindfolds MACK)* "The great Egyptian age is but a remnant of the Atlantean culture The antediluvian kings colonized the world. All the gods who play in the mythological dramas in all legends from all lands were from fair Atlantis. Knowing her fate, Atlantis sent out ships to all corners of the world. On board were the twelve The poet, the physician, the farmer, the scientist, the magician and the other so-called gods of our legends, though gods they were. And as the elders of our time choose to remain blind, let us rejoice and let us sing and dance and ring in the new. That's what it is.

MACK: So that's what it is.

PEGEEN: Yes.

MACK: Are we going to burn?

PEGEEN: Oh yes we are.

KIRSTEN: But we can't.

PEGEEN: Oh, we will and it'll be okay.

DOC: Let's get out while we can.

PEGEEN: Stay where you are.

CORTEZ: Don't move.

DOC: But I don't want to burn.

PRODUCER: You want to burn.

KIRSTEN: We have to stay in the house and don't be afraid.

CORTEZ: Be brave now.

PEGEEN: Stay still.

PRODUCER: Lead us not into temptation.

(Cut)

(CORTEZ sits at small table, smoking and taking notes KIRSTEN sits opposite. MACK remains laying on table.)

DOC: Now you've learned.

KIRSTEN: Get me out of here. I want to go to Pittsburgh.

CORTEZ: And from the bottom of my heart I deeply resent your miscalculated implication.

PRODUCER: Direct hit.

CORTEZ: It's eroding everything. Corroding it.

MACK: A flaming hysteric.

DOC: I am not a flaming hysteric.

PRODUCER: Flaming.

KIRSTEN:A long time ago, someone told me this would happen and it has happened and you'll accept it.

PEGEEN: I can see bright burning days ahead of you. Bright glowing days all around you. Do you need something?

PRODUCER: Yes.

KIRSTEN: Look in my eyes. Do you see it? Look.

PEGEEN: Look harder.

KIRSTEN:. I see a dark lonely corner inside your eye.

PRODUCER: That's it.

CORTEZ: And a body rotting in a dark deep hole at the bottom of your eye.

MACK: A broken body down at the end of it.

KIRSTEN: Keep looking. Do you see anything beyond it?

PEGEEN: Keep looking, don't look away.

KIRSTEN: Keep looking.

PEGEEN: Keep looking. Don't be afraid, don't be afraid.

MACK: I don't even know what you're talking about.

KIRSTEN: I'm not talking.

CORTEZ: I see a heavy trail of broken heads and they're all ours. Burned, charred heads and they're all ours.

PRODUCER: They're all ours.

KIRSTEN: Stop shuddering.

PEGEEN: Stay calm.

DOC: Intervene.

MACK: Intercede.

PEGEEN: You will find your endless and impenetrable love in my eye, at the bottom of my eye and it will serve you forever and no one can deny the love within my eye

KIRSTEN: I see bright burning days ahead of you but the fire won't hurt you. You won't feel the flames. You'll feel the flames but there will be no pain. Keep your eye on the sparrow.

PEGEEN: The fire is getting brighter and hotter but you won't feel it. Keep listening to my voice. The fire will burn for three days but you won't feel it because you'll be ash.

KIRSTEN: And you will finally blow out through the top of my head in a blinding light.

PEGEEN: You belong to me and I belong to you and we all belong to each other.

DOC: And the cowboys will be slaughtered with their cattle and the Indians will chain their bodies into the hot sun and dry them into dust.

KIRSTEN: This house will burn but the lion will sleep.

PEGEEN: Hush my darling, don't fear my darling, the lion sleeps tonight.

MACK: Where are we?

KIRSTEN: I told you.

CORTEZ: The spring is spewing forth into us. The sky is falling in on us.

MACK: So what.

PRODUCER: The clouds are on fire and the sky is falling, so big deal.

MACK: Are they going to burn us?

PEGEEN: Oh, yes. They're going to bum us and there's no coincidence.

DOC: Who is burning us?

KIRSTEN: Oh, everyone is burning us. The left and the right. The top and the bottom. East and west and north and south.

PEGEEN: Old and young and middle age.

MACK: But why?

KIRSTEN: When you have a fire in your hand you have to keep it burning and you keep it burning something.

DOC: Anything.

MACK: It's a lie.

CORTEZ: The rain will put it out.

DOC: No it won't.

CORTEZ: The rain is on fire.

MACK: The water is on fire and so it won't put it out.

DOC: You didn't tell me that water was flammable.

MACK: So.

PRODUCER: You never drank it.

CORTEZ: It's not water. It's gasoline. Clean clear and pure octane.

DOC: Sweet petroleum extract.

MACK: But the spring.

PEGEEN: It isn't a spring. It's an oil well, a gusher.

MACK: So.

PRODUCER: But it was so clear.

CORTEZ: It was as black as night. A tar pit full of dead bog people rotting in their own tarry simulacra after twenty decades.

MACK: Where's the lady now?

PEGEEN: I'm here. She'd never leave us.

MACK: Tell her to get out.

CORTEZ: She can't. What can she do? The water's turned to gasoline. It'll only make it hotter. But she's smiling. Pray.

PEGEEN: I guess you could say that we have been lucky or we have not been lucky.

CORTEZ: Bullshit.

DOC: That stupid, glittering, critical moment of supreme crucifixion will vanish away from you.

MACK: You know you never will.

CORTEZ: How do I believe all this?

PRODUCER: You know you never will.

MACK: I am absent, a conduit, a funnel and I hate symbols. A lightning rod, an android, a figment, a robot, a misconception, a fucking asshole.

PRODUCER: A dumb machine. A universe constructed already Constructible, indestructible.

KIRSTEN: Not a good question.

CORTEZ: It'll kill me.

PEGEEN: You will depend on me.

DOC: Does it have anything to do with love?

KIRSTEN: Oh, I would hope so.

MACK: How so?

PEGEEN: There, do you see it? There's a tiny little flame in the sky over there.

MACK: I don't see it.

PEGEEN: Yes you do.

(Cut)

(Actors remain in place in darkness. On ambient monitors, night shot of glowing window.)

KIRSTEN: And are you aware that you murdered the two from the talk show?

CORTEZ: Well, they burned in the house. It was the fire.

KIRSTEN: Why couldn't they get out?

CORTEZ: Well, they could have gotten out but the fire caught them.

KIRSTEN: The fire caught them because they couldn't get out.
CORTEZ: Correct.
KIRSTEN: And why couldn't they get out?
CORTEZ: I locked the doors.
KIRSTEN: What about the windows?
CORTEZ: There were no windows.
KIRSTEN: So they burned.
CORTEZ: Yes, they did. They seemed like they didn't mind it. But the water should have put it out. I kept pouring more and more.
KIRSTEN: That was gasoline.
CORTEZ: I thought it was water.
KIRSTEN: I decided a long time ago when I was a small child that I would see something like this. That I would take it upon myself to see it, that I would conjure an event and that I would enlist you into my services. My little army. And that from there we would continue on into our own and that it wouldn't be a heresy that would insult people.

CORTEZ: How can you say this? You're only a child.
MACK: And does it have anything to do with love?

KIRSTEN: Oh, yes I would hope so. Yes indeed.

MACK: And that I wouldn't be diabolical about it like as if I was a murderer or something and that you could see into my mind. That I would let you see into my mind, into my pain into my happiness into my love for all of you and that because of that you would believe me because you could see all of my pain and stigmata constantly bleeding with love and pain.

CORTEZ: And that all this would go around you in a circle and keep you safe from the things you believe and that it would not interrupt your thinking or feeling of anything or any other kind of reality which you might be or might want to be a part of. That it would be an odorless, smokeless, harmless, invisible and indivisible.

KIRSTEN: And that you would take me and have me and love me into your heart of hearts with your mind standing by waiting and watching and thinking.

CORTEZ: Does it have anything to do with love?

KIRSTEN: That's a good question

MACK: But I think I've answered it. That you wouldn't think of me as some kind of mystical idiot And that we would risk everything. The home, the car, the boat. Everything but the kids.

CORTEZ: A sacrifice, a sacrilege.

KIRSTEN: But what do you really think about it?

MACK: I don't think anything. I made it up. It's not to be thought about.

KIRSTEN: Oh, yes it is. If I could force myself to force the thought like a broken glass through my forehead and out of my hands. I am only a simulacra, an ideology, a dialectic, the water table, poisoned water wells, a hippie dream.

CORTEZ: Let's go to Philadelphia.

KIRSTEN: Don't mind him. I told you he was a hysteric.

MACK: Well, do something about him. You're a priest Can't you do anything?

CORTEZ: What do you want me to do? Hear his confession? Put a spell on him? Give him extreme unction?

(Cut)

(MACK and DOC remain in place.)

CORTEZ: No.

MACK: Sit on that bench and shut up. Sit on that bench and shut up, I said.

KIRSTEN: What's that on there?

DOC: What?

KIRSTEN: That faint stain.

MACK: Blood

DOC: From what?

- 219 -

MACK: I don't know.

KIRSTEN: Should we wash it?

MACK: No, I like it. If it's there it belongs there permanently. Forever.

KIRSTEN: Was it real what you saw?

MACK: I don't mean it wasn't real. It was real.

CORTEZ: What was real?

MACK: The lady in the ball.

CORTEZ: And why is she doing this?

MACK: I don't know.

KIRSTEN: Didn't she tell you?

MACK: No.

CORTEZ: Didn't she say she wanted a church?

MACK: I never saw anything.

KIRSTEN: Didn't she say to call a priest?

MACK: I never saw anything.

CORTEZ: Didn't she tell you to pray?

KIRSTEN: Drink the water.

MACK:. These thorns are killing me.

KIRSTEN: Drink the water.

MACK: That's not water. You're trying to tempt me with alcohol.

CORTEZ: Do you have anything to confess?

MACK: I have nothing to confess.

KIRSTEN: Everything you've seen is true.

CORTEZ: Everything I've seen is true.

MACK: Except that it's not really true I never saw it.

That's all I have to say. Or I thought I saw it and the more I was asked the more I saw it but now I don't see anything. I never saw anything.

KIRSTEN: Drink the water

MACK: What's in this? You're poisoning me. I know it. Get it out of here. No one leaves this room. Who was it? Who's trying to poison me?

CORTEZ: Put the knife down. Put it down.

MACK: There's something in here I know it. You're poisoning me. Shall we pray?

(Cut)

(KIRSTEN,DOC, MACK remain in place. Day window on all monitors.)

KIRSTEN: We only want to see what you see. Like you see. That's all.

MACK: Why?

DOC: Does it matter to you if I see what you see or if I believe you?

MACK: No. Maybe it's only for my eyes, for my eyes only, only for us to see.

KIRSTEN: Us?

MACK: Me and I.

DOC: Are you sad at all about this?

MACK: No.

KIRSTEN: Are you pretending any of this?

MACK: No. Sometimes when I see something.

KIRSTEN: You will see what I see and how I see it. And I will see what you see and if my world falls apart before my eyes, your world will fall apart before your eyes and we will both see the same and whatever is there we will both or all three see together. Our six eyes will be one eye. We'll all be one eye, see out of one eye. Whether it is deliberately or not, it is just one eye and we will all see out of it. You're only part of a machine, our machine and because you are part of it, we'll all work together whether you want to or not. We will all see the same things together.

MACK: Everything that comes out of my mouth is a lie.

KIRSTEN: Everything that goes into my eye is exactly what is there. Left or right, right or wrong.

DOC: What about the lady?

KIRSTEN: She's the center of the machine. We know the answer is yes. And we can see every moment exactly. Every obscurity. Its dissolving qualities and reflection on the ceiling. The whole shooting match.

(Cut)

(Actors remain in darkness. Day window on ambient monitors.)

CORTEZ: *As I was saying to the sky the other day. My love is unspeakable, undeniable, indelible, inalienable, indivisible, shimmering. But though I love you with a love true, who can cling to a rambling rose?*

MACK: *Do you think you were made by anything? Initiated, created, put together, thought up, instigated, appropriated, pieced together, conceived?*

CORTEZ: These thorns are killing me.

KIRSTEN: Though I love you with a love true, who can cling to a rambling rose? So I will not cling anymore.

MACK: These thorns are killing me.

KIRSTEN: Look in here. What are you seeing?

MACK: Watery.

KIRSTEN: You're looking at the inside of your own eye. What do you see?

MACK: Just something watery.

KIRSTEN: Do you see anything else? Anything floating in it?

MACK: A desert made out of water.

CORTEZ: That's what I saw. Now you see what 1 saw in my eye.

KIRSTEN: Are you happy with what you see or not so happy with what you see?

CORTEZ: I'm afraid.

KIRSTEN: They will hand your head to you on a plate surrounded by rambling roses burning.

CORTEZ: Why?

KIRSTEN: Why do you want to know everything? Why do you have to know everything? Why do you have to want to know everything? Everything on earth for God's sake. Does it satisfy you if I said I am the walrus? I don't care if you really saw it or not or if it was really there or not. I just want to know if you were telling the truth about whatever it was. That's the most important thing here, right now in this minute before it passes. I'm going to give you till the morning comes.

MACK: Too late.

KIRSTEN: And you will believe me and be convinced not because of what I say but because of how I say it.

CORTEZ: How many people are in this room.?

MACK: Six.

KIRSTEN: Watch closely now. Six divided by two is three. Divided by two is one and a half If six was nine divided by two is four and a half divided by two or any other number is two and a quarter so you see any other way you look at it there is only one person in this room. 1 tried so hard to tell you last night. You wouldn't talk to me. Sooner or later one of us must know that all you see around yourself is yourself. Everything you see around you is yourself and you're not your brother's keeper because there's no brother to keep but yourself and so if that is true, is it true that you saw that lady?

MACK: I told you. What does it matter if those people got cured, right or wrong?

KIRSTEN: Because if you're right then I'm right and if you're wrong then I'm wrong. One chair, one table, one TV, one each of everything.

MACK: But they are cured aren't they?

KIRSTEN: Yes. Doctors have testified they are.

MACK: Why?

KIRSTEN: I don't know why.

MACK: You mean to tell me they're cured and you don't know why?

KIRSTEN: I'm not a doctor.

MACK: My eyes hurt.

KIRSTEN:I am not a doctor. Watch closely now.
CORTEZ: How many people are there in this
room?
MACK: Six.
KIRSTEN: How many?
MACK: Three.
KIRSTEN: How many people are there in this
room?
MACK: Two.
KIRSTEN: Who?
MACK: You and me.
KIRSTEN: How many people are in this room?
MACK: One.
KIRSTEN: Who is it?
MACK: Me.
KIRSTEN: There, do you see it? There's a tiny little
flame lighting in the sky over there. Do you see it?
MACK: Yes.
KIRSTEN: Who is it?
MACK: Me.

(All video monitors go out.)

END OF PLAY

BLACK MARIA

Photo credit: Dayton Taylor

BLACK MARIA was first projected at the La Mama Annex, NYC on April 8, 1987 with the following cast:

Larry Tighe	*STONE, X*
Black-Eyed Susan	*CALVADOS*
Jane Smith	*JANE*
Sanghi Wagner	*ESTHER*
Helena White	*CATLIN*
Jun Maeda	*MANGAS*
Michael Tighe	*WANDER*

Text ,direction, design- John Jesurun
Production Manager: Brad Phillips

Cinematography,Technical Director,Line Producer: Richard Connors

Cinematography: Kurt Rosen

Sound: Jim Coleman

Edit: John Jesurun, Richard Connors

Props: Jun Maeda

Characters:

WANDER: Twelve years old
CALVADOS: Mid forties
STONE: Mid forties
ESTHER: Early thirties
JANE: Late seventies
MANGAS: Mid forties
CATLIN: Seventeen years old
X: Middle aged man's voice

(Five 15x20 ft. screens surround the audience on four sides and above. Five synchronized 16mm films are rear projected on these screens.

1.*(Scene begins in darkness. A light bulb on the top screen brightens to reveal ALL sitting along the four sides of a stone room. Unless otherwise indicated, all are shabbily dressed and have dirty faces and hair. Laughter.)*

WANDER: What are you doing?! What are you doing?!
ESTHER: What do you want from me?
WANDER: Why are you doing this ?
ESTHER: Listen to me, I'm telling you something.
WANDER: What are you doing?

ESTHER: So that you'll learn the value of suffering, The joy of sacrifice and patience, murder and manslaughter. So that you'll learn to speak the language of the dead. Once again it's time for you to shut up. Belly up to the buzzsaw, gravitational collapse, Blackleg, Yankee pot roast. Stop crying. You should be happy. Listen to me, I'm telling you something. You tell someone else and they'll tell someone else. Would you like a radio to listen to?
CATLIN: Yes.
ESTHER: This is what the horse told me. This is his suicide note, his poison-pen letter. First, I'll give the clue, then the story,then the real story. First what they saw, then what was seen, then what was. The cadaver will direct the autopsy, A talking corpse narrating. A dead horse talking,
WANDER: What are you trying to tell me?
ESTHER: Don't give me the ching-chang yip-yap.
STONE: I don't like it in here.
CALVADOS: I don't either.
JANE: I don't know what's the matter with him.
ESTHER: You move one foot of bed and you're a dead man. That horse is dead. I was looking at it outside. It had one fly on it. But that fly was tiny, triumphant. You have been found neither guilty nor innocent but you have been found. Stop crying.

CATLIN: What's that dripping?

ESTHER: Blood, urine, pieces of marijuana, Carbon monoxide.

WANDER: Why did you put us in here?

ESTHER: I'm sorry that you're dead, alright?

STONE: Alright.

ESTHER: Once again it's time for you to shut up. Don't touch the circuit breaker.

CALVADOS: What's that moving?

ESTHER: A salamander come to eat the turnips. I had wanted to tell you about my deep and unrelenting and unequivocal disbelief and unbelief in everything. But now I've changed my mind. Do you understand that? Oh, how I cannot bear the thought of you. You know, that's from a song.

JANE: What's that dripping?

ESTHER: Crocodile tears. I'd like to read a nice book now and then with a story in the middle that goes nowhere. Don't you understand? You've been murdered, killed. Your head hit a bullet. Habeas corpus, a talking corpse. You were lost but now you're found. I found you. You're pulverized, a smoke signal, a cat dream, a Molly Maguire.

STONE: I can't hear anything.

ESTHER: You're fuckin' brain dead, that's why. A pack of flies is riding around in your head. That fly was tiny, triumphant. I promise.

JANE: Morning yet?

WANDER: Hold the room still, will you?

ESTHER: This is my room. It's beautiful. It's always beautiful. I love it. Here's the record player. I call the room Black Maria because at night it gets so dark you don't know where you are. In the day it's hell, but at night, when everyone is asleep, it's heaven.

CALVADOS: I don't want to stay here.

ESTHER: Yes, you do. I'll leave the gun here with you. You can use it if you want. But wait for one night and you won't want to use it. In the day you'll feel like using it but at night you won't. The horse loved it in here. Then you put me in here. Mushrooms grow here at night and you can eat them. You'll see so many things in this room you won't want to leave it. You'll be married to it. You won't know where the room begins and you end. Let me see your hand. It's afraid. Don't you like it in here ?

JANE: Are we in somewhere?

CATLIN: What's that smell?

ESTHER: Sour mash, camphor, apple rotting.

WANDER: Is that puppet dead?

ESTHER: No. Would you like a book?

JANE: I read that book backwards and forwards and every time I read it, it says something different.

CATLIN: Open the window.

ESTHER: Why are you here?

STONE: To buy the horse.

ESTHER: Why don't you get out of here? There's no horse here. Let me tell you honestly there is no horse here. But I have a gun and we can share it.

CALVADOS: I don't want to.

ESTHER: Share the gun. You take it and keep it.

WANDER: Don't take it.

ESTHER: Stop arguing. What are you waiting for? Can you see the gun ? You can only see it from one point in the room. Who can see it? Whoever can see it can have it. Who can see it? No one? One person can see the gun. No? So I built a house of cards to keep warm and I got inside my house of cards and burnt it. And it kept me warm for a while. A good long while. I found that if I kept talking and kept very still, I'd stay warm. But then it got very lonely in that house. People shouldn't be alone. And I thought, I have these mushrooms and if I can share them maybe it won't be so lonely. So I tried to share them with the birds. But no one wanted to share them so I ate them and threw the gun into a river. And then what did you do ?

WANDER: I got caught in a projector and then I became very religious. Maybe you can help me.

ESTHER: What can I do for you?

STONE:I was under the impression that the horse would be black.

ESTHER: No. No black horses here. Very hard to find. So what did you do?

(Silence)

What did you do?

(Silence)

Don't just sit there breathing, You should be having the time of your life.

CUT

2. (*ALL sitting in an open stable area.*)

X: A long time ago in pariah times I was living in a leper colony. I had lost the sensation in my eyes and I had to translate for a speech defect person, which was my job before the leper colony where I had gone to buy a horse. They raised the best, very rare and precious. And I had to hear everything through a microscope. Virtually everyone mentioned in this book is alive and intellectually still active.

CALVADOS: How are you?

X: I'm fine.

JANE: The sky stays the same, always the same, the sky doesn't change.

CALVADOS: I had for awhile some very difficult difficulty remembering bad memories of good memories and good memories of bad memories.

X: But let me start at the beginning.

CATLIN: Oh, please, not again.

WANDER: We didn't even have to look in no mirrors to see how dry and scratched up our faces had gotten and become.

JANE: And my Mississippi homeland is burnt up like a shred, a deformed adventure.
STONE: And our language over the days had gotten mis-sewn and misshapen and misunderstood, not understood no more.
CATLIN: But we're pretty tranquil here.
X: What's the matter with all of you?
WANDER: We're the red rainbow gang.
JANE: A tobacco road beheading.
CALVADOS: Yes, all those things.
WANDER: Eventually you'll fit into a tablespoon.
X: Flies will ride herd on you.
CALVADOS: But you'll still be full of light inside.
JANE: My poor baby, it was a midget basking in the dead sun.
CALVADOS: Nothing we could do but burn it and bury it. It was so frail.
X: I just want to get the facts straight.
CATLIN: Ain't no straight facts.
WANDER: They're playing that same movie on TV again.
CATLIN: This is where there's a skirmish at the picnic.
WANDER: And the cat dreams he's a horse. But why would a cat dream, mommy ? Why would a cat dream? Why would it ? It just don't seem right, it just don't seem right.
JANE: Something in its sub-conciousness.
WANDER: But why would a cat dream ?

STONE: Something in its subconscious, dear.

WANDER: How many times do I have to ask?

CALVADOS: Just watch the TV.

CATLIN: The movie's ending.

WANDER: Oh, don't end it. Please don't end it, please don't !

STONE: We are under the impression that Europe died in the Second World War.

CALVADOS: Suicide as it were.

CATLIN: Hell to pay.

CALVADOS: Stop licking your wounds. I can't get that dog to stop.

JANE: A long time ago when we were living in pariah times I was living in a leper colony. I had lost the sensation in my eyes and I had to translate for a speech defect person.

X: And I told them. "You will have to suffer, there's nothing I can do for you, not a thing I can do. You'll have to hear through a microscope so that you can pretend that very small sounds are very big instead of very big sounds being very small. Do you understand? You will have to hear through your fingertips and ignore the blood falling through your ears. Do you understand? And think of me as a pinhole camera. That's all I have to go by. A pinhole of light coming through. My pinhole and your ear microscope together."

JANE: Dreary.

CALVADOS: Your ears are so small and frail.

X: Don't you understand? I can't help you, there's nothing I can do anymore. Your ears are poisoned and I'm seeing through a pinhole. There's nothing I can do anymore.

CATLIN: Do you know any folk songs?

WANDER: You talk like a cottonmouth.

JANE: Don't be rude.

CALVADOS: We got cottonmouth in the lake.

CATLIN: They come out in water.

WANDER: Skate on the lake.

X: I bet.

CALVADOS: Eat up.

X ; What is this?

CALVADOS: Fresh cottonmouth.

CATLIN: Kilt it today.

WANDER: The hogs had just eaten and devoured a new born deer fawn. They gorged themselves and I had been huntin' fawn all day.

CATLIN: And those damn hogs had just eaten the whole thing.

WANDER:I shot that hog. Fuckin' peccary. And I left it layin' there luxuriating in a sea of its own vomit, fuckin' peccary.

CATLIN: Hog's head luxuriating in a sea of its own vomit.

CALVADOS: Granny does your dog bite?

JANE: Eat up.

WANDER: That's when I saw the cotton mouth slide up out of the lake.

CATLIN: So I shot it.

WANDER: Fuckin' peccary.
STONE: Fuckin' peccary.
JANE: Eat up.
CALVADOS: And enough stories.
X: Why don't you eat the hogs?
CALVADOS: Never eat hogs.
STONE: That true, pig boy?
WANDER: Don't call me that.
STONE: Why not ?
WANDER: Don't call me pig boy. Ain't no pig
boy.
CATLIN: And they ain't no pigs, they're
peccary.
WANDER: Wild boar.
STONE: Which is what you are.
WANDER: Wild boar, pig hog.
X: Happy child.
WANDER: Ain't no child, I'm twenty five.
STONE: Then you shrunk.
WANDER: Twenty-five.
CATLIN: Teen dust head.
WANDER: Twenty-five.
STONE: Dust head.
WANDER: I'll shoot you and put you with that
gorged pig in a pit.
CALVADOS: This pit viper is delicious.
CATLIN: I shot it myself so be grateful and
don't insult.
JANE: You should know better.
WANDER: I know better than to eat pit viper.
CATLIN: Ain't no pit viper. Cottonmouth.

CALVADOS: Know any folk songs?

JANE: I hate folk songs.

X: What can you sing ?

JANE: Anything.

CALVADOS: She don't sing no more ever since.

X: Ever since what?

CALVADOS: Just ever since.

WANDER: Now eat your pit viper, it's getting cold.

CATLIN: Pomegranates for desert.

CALVADOS: Fresh off the tree, not a mark on them.

JANE: This pomegranate is just so.....

CUT

(*ESTHER sits inside a small wooden one room house. CALVADOS sits just outside. Mountains in the distance. Birds sing.*)

X: Why have they put you in here?

ESTHER: Why did they put me in here? Because people are w   eird I guess.

X: That's no reason.

ESTHER: It's reason enough for them.

X: Well, I'll let you out.

ESTHER: No use.

X: Why no use?

ESTHER: Because I broke out of here so many times but they always catch me and find me.

X: Why they put you in here?

ESTHER: Because they're weird. I told you.

X: Why?

ESTHER: They say I killed somebody.

X: Did you?

ESTHER: Maybe.

CALVADOS: Maybe.

ESTHER: Besides, it doesn't matter. I like it in here.

X: Well, if you killed someone, why don't they just send you away?

ESTHER: This is their way of sending me away. It's the way they like to punish. They get pleasure from it.

X: You don't like it in here.

ESTHER: No.

X: There's no lock on the door.

ESTHER: Yes, there is. It's alright. They come visit me sometimes and we talk. They bring me records. Will you buy the horse?

X: I'll have to wait and see.

ESTHER: It's a nice horse.

CALVADOS: I told you not to talk to her.

X: Why?

CALVADOS: She crazy, she can hurt you.

X ; With what?

CALVADOS: She'll find something, she's crazy weird, she kill and scalp.

X: Come off it.

ESTHER: No.

X: What are you looking at?

ESTHER: Nothing. There's a horse out there I want to buy.

X: Buy with what?

ESTHER: I'm going to buy it with the gun.

X: Alright.

ESTHER: Can I go?

CALVADOS: No.

ESTHER: Have you seen the rats in here? I've been making friends with them. Everyday I'm very silent, immovable and I let them come closer and feed them a little bit of bread day by day and now they're my friends. At first they were timid but now they eat out of my hands and sleep near me and cuddle at night.

CALVADOS: There aren't any rats in here.

ESTHER: Yes, there are. They won't come out because they don't know you and if they did they wouldn't like you. They know you're the prison guard. So I'm here to stay.

CALVADOS: I'm going and I'm never coming back. How long are you staying?

X: Long enough to see if the horse is any good.

CALVADOS: For what?

X: To ride.

CALVADOS: It's no good, get out. You come to the wrong place.

X: Why are they locked up in there like that.

CALVADOS: They got to stay there.

X: Why?

CALVADOS: They're all crazy and killers.

X: Why are they locked in there?

CALVADOS: Because if they don't get locked up, they get out and turn into crazy killers. This is a prison.

X: For what, why?

CALVADOS: Get out.

ESTHER: Get out.

CALVADOS: They want to hurt you, so get out. You're getting them all mixed up, so get out!

CUT

(*CALVADOS, ESTHER, CATLIN sit on three sides of the open stable area. WANDER sits above them in a window sized roof section open to the sky.*)

CALVADOS:...after I was overcome by the smoke.

X: What happened?

CALVADOS: I was overcome by the smoke. I have no idea.

ESTHER: Keep the room dark, keep it dark I said. Don't put the light on, don't. I like it dark. I'm a mushroom and I like it dark. I don't want to see anything. I've seen enough, I don't want to see no more. If you turn on that light I'll kill you.

X: With what?

CALVADOS: A mushroom.

ESTHER: I'll kill you, I said. It's dark. You don't know what I have in my hand.

WANDER: What could you kill me with? Your rosary? I bit that to pieces.

CALVADOS: The record player.

CATLIN: You could konk me on the head with it and knock me out.

CALVADOS: She could have broken one of the records and sharpened it into a knife.

CATLIN: Be careful.

ESTHER: Close that door and leave the light off. You light a match and you're a dead pair of quails.

CATLIN: Ok, alright.

ESTHER: Now get out and leave me alone in here!

CALVADOS: But we want to let you out.

ESTHER: No, you don't.

CALVADOS: We do.

ESTHER: I don't want to stay in here but I like it.

CATLIN: Why?

ESTHER: I like it in the dark. What am I wearing?

CATLIN: Nothing.

ESTHER: Wrong.

X: You're naked.

ESTHER: No, I'm not.

X: I can feel the warmth of your body. I can feel the fumes of heat coming off it.

ESTHER: No, you can't.

X: Yes, I can.

CATLIN: Don't be a maniac please.

ESTHER: Just let me shoot you.

CALVADOS: No.

ESTHER: Let me shoot you.

CATLIN: Don't mess.

ESTHER: I will mess. You're going to shoot me anyway.

CATLIN: So shoot.

CALVADOS: Don't mess.

ESTHER: Mess. I can hear your heart beating.

X: No, you cant.

ESTHER: I can hear your heart beating. You're scared aren't you?

CALVADOS: You can't hear it.

ESTHER: I can hear your heart beating. Are you scared? I can see it beating there on the floor.

X: You can not.

ESTHER: You're afraid. Do you think I'm afraid to kill you? Well, I'm not.

X: Why are you doing this? I didn't do nothing.

ESTHER: Yes, you did and now you've got to go. (*All four side screens pan to right and Esther disappears from one screen. JANE and CATLIN are revealed together on another. STONE and CALVADOS on another. CATLIN chews on an apple.*)

WANDER: Did you hear about the flood watch? (*WANDER, on top screen, jumps in through ceiling opening and appears on the floor of a side screen.*)

CALVADOS: There's a red flag down on the riverbank.

CATLIN: I climbed the tree. I saw it.

STONE: So what.

WANDER: We got to go to high ground.

STONE: That's no flood watch.

JANE: Who is that guy?

STONE: Escaped convict, murderer convict. He's thirsty.

CALVADOS: Where is he?

CATLIN: He's in the hen house.

CALVADOS: Get him out of there, the chickens!

WANDER: He says he know about flood watch. He's used to defendin' flood towns.

CATLIN: This ain't no flood town.

STONE: Self defense.

JANE: What are you scared of?

CATLIN: He's no escaped murderer.

CALVADOS: Why is he alone?

WANDER: He come to buy the horse.

JANE: With what money?

CALVADOS: He got no money.

STONE: Murderers are always alone. That's why they're murderers, they kill everyone and then they're alone. They travel alone, they got to, got no other choice. And now he's going to kill us because he got to be alone.

JANE: He likes to be alone and so he's got to kill us.

CALVADOS: He got no other choice.

STONE: We got no other choice but to kill him.

WANDER: Kill him in the hen house and bury the guy.

STONE: Where's that gun?

CALVADOS: Don't kill him.

CATLIN: He's no escaped murderer.

WANDER: Self defense.

STONE: He's a Baskerville, be careful.

JANE: Now get with it.

CALVADOS: He's a Baskerville.

WANDER: You're disinformationin' everything, little sister.

CALVADOS: Then who is he?

CATLIN: We know who he is, he come to buy the horse.

CALVADOS: He's thirsty, he stay a few days to try the horse again.

WANDER. No.

JANE: You think you're in some big blue sky western.

WANDER: No.

STONE: You're a pig in the night, pipe down.

WANDER: I seen him snooping around.

STONE: Where?

WANDER: Down where the spiders cry.

JANE: Where's my pillow?

CATLIN: Get it and get under it.

JANE: Where is he now?

CALVADOS: On the hill where the pigs stand still.

JANE: Where's that?

WANDER: Where the chuck wagon race was.
CATLIN: Where the three horses died in the chuck wagon race.
JANE: That was a hundred years ago.
CALVADOS: Three had to be destroyed, shot in the head.
STONE: Stampeded with bullets.
WANDER: They was ugly as burnt rope when we finished with them.
STONE: Watch his lips. If they're moving he's lying.
WANDER: I don't remember that chuck wagon race.
STONE: Go show him the horse.
WANDER: It's my horse.
CALVADOS: It's our horse.
STONE: If he's a murderer we'll put his neck on the block.
CATLIN: But I don't think so.
JANE: You got all the wrong information based on wrong facts.
WANDER: Then what's he lookin' for out there?
CALVADOS: He just walkin'.
STONE: In search of holy hell or something.
WANDER: Then he come to the right shanty.
JANE: He's a nice guy.
CATLIN: He don't look too weird.
WANDER: He's a murderer I tell you. Some kind of weird Chiricaua bully- boy.
CALVADOS: Rock steady, Pinnochio head!

WANDER: Isn't it true that…
CUT
(JANE, CATLIN and WANDER on separate screens looking out windows on foggy winter landscape.)

JANE: And he had the dead fawn strapped to his chest and dragged it all the way down the prairie and fell on it and killed it again even though it was already dead.
CATLIN: And then he laid down on his head and kicked the habit. Just kicked it.
WANDER: Pretty funky.
CATLIN: There were these little gray winds blowing all around out there.
WANDER: Its scary.
CATLIN: Where's the gun?
WANDER: Which one?
CATLIN: Any one.
WANDER: Get it out and shoot. Give a shot out there, just anywhere.
CATLIN: Where?
WANDER: Just anywhere.
CATLIN: Alright. *(She points a large pistol out the window and shoots.)*
JANE: Don't mess.
WANDER: What?
JANE: Don't mess. I said, don't mess.
CATLIN: Alright, I won't mess but shall I shoot?

WANDER: Shoot, shoot! (*He shoots a large pistol into the camera. The camera lens cracks.*)
CATLIN: Anything?
JANE: No.
WANDER: There's a dog barking out there.
CATLIN: Barking.
WANDER: Barking his head off.
CATLIN: Shoot!
WANDER: Any more barking?
CATLIN: Did you hit it?
WANDER: Yes.
CATLIN: Is it dead?
WANDER: How would I know if it's dead? It's dark out there.
CATLIN: I just must have hit it. My luck.
WANDER: Maybe it was a heat seeking bullet.
CATLIN: No, just luck.
WANDER: Its probably bleeding to death out there.
CATLIN: Do you hear any whimpering?
WANDER: Then it must be dead.
CATLIN: As a doornail.
WANDER: It's probably bleeding to death out there.
CATLIN: We'll go out in the morning and pick it up and bury it.
WANDER: Alright.
CATLIN: We don't want the flies to get at it and cause a putrefaction.
WANDER: Go out in the morning and bury it.
CATLIN: Alright.

WANDER: Good night.

CATLIN: If it's not dead it'll probably turn into a goon and git us tonight...

WANDER: ...come in and strangle us and scratch us to death with its claws.

CATLIN: Not if we keep the fire on.

WANDER: Goons are scared of fire so put another log on.

CATLIN: It'll probably come in the middle of the night like some Apache renegade and scratch us all up to pieces.

WANDER: Who cares, it's probably dead and limping half way to hell by now.

CATLIN: I can smell it burning. Its hair is all singe-ing off. So there's nothing to be afraid.

WANDER: It'll probably come back as a bitter fruit and poison us.

CATLIN: So what, good night.

CUT

(*The empty shell of an abandoned stone house with no floors or roof. CATLIN and WANDER sit in the empty second floor windowsills. STONE, JANE,MANGAS,CALVADOS stand or sit among the ruins.*)

X: Who are all these people?

CALVADOS: Refugees from a wagon train.

X: Come off it. What are you doing here?

CALVADOS: The wagon train was attacked by Indians.

X: And you ran away?

WANDER: There aren't any Indians around here, we killed them all.

CALVADOS: Except one and we have her in the basement house.

X: What's she doing in there?

CALVADOS: She's a prisoner.

X: For what?

CALVADOS: For killing and scalping my father and mother. Who could blame her?

WANDER: That's true but she's been in there for two years and we ain't lettin' her out.

JANE: Cut that phony accent.

WANDER: Ok, but she's a scalper and we have her trapped.

X: Lets see her.

CALVADOS: Why? You might recognize her.

X: Maybe.

CATLIN: She don't look like no Indian.

JANE: Cut that accent, I said.

WANDER: She don't look like no Indian, I said.

X: Are you one?

ESTHER: Of course not.

CALVADOS: She can't speak English.

STONE: Why should she?

CATLIN: You ain't no Indian.

ESTER: Oh, how I cannot bear the thought of you.

X: Can you drive a car?

ESTHER: Yes.

X: Can you ride a horse?

ESTHER: No.

CALVADOS: Thought so.

ESTHER: I had a car but they took it.

X: Is that the car outside?

ESTHER: Yes, it's my car.

WANDER: Who ever heard of an Indian with a car?!

ESTHER: It's my car.

CALVADOS: Oh, Jesus!

CATLIN: Why she in here for so long?

CALVADOS: She's prisoner, I told you.

X: But why?

STONE: For scalping.

ESTHER: I didn't scalp no one.

WANDER: You did too.

CALVADOS: You certainly tried.

STONE: She pull a knife on me.

CATLIN: You pull a knife on him?

ESTHER: Yes.

X: Why?

ESTHER: I try to cut him.

X: Why?

ESTHER: I try to cut him, kill him 'cause he put me in here.

CATLIN: Why he put you in here?

ESTHER: Because he say I try to cut him but he drag me from my car and try to shoot my foot off, he crazy.

X: That true?

STONE: No, she try to scalp my mom and pop.

X: Where they?
WANDER: They both dead.
X: How?
CATLIN: She cut them up and kill them.
X: Why ?
WANDER: She crazy girl.
CALVADOS: You crazy girl.
ESTHER: No, I just drive my car by here and they shoot the tire out and try to kill me on the road.
CATLIN: We did not.
ESTHER: They try to kill me on the road, they put me down here and try to scare me into saying I kill his family.
STONE: You crazy girl.
ESTHER: Horse mouth.
STONE: Boar's head.
ESTHER: Horse hoof.
STONE: She cut them up and kill them.
CATLIN: She kill no one.
STONE: You shut up.
CATLIN: She kill no one.
ESTHER: First I shut you up, then I cut you up.
WANDER: You crazy girl.
ESTHER: I'm not crazy , they put me in here.
X: These people try and get pleasure from you?
ESTHER: These people couldn't get pleasure out of a bag of bones or a doorknob.
STONE: They don't know what pleasure is.
WANDER: You crazy girl.

ESTHER: They get pleasure alright by putting me in here.
X: But why?
CATLIN: Who the hell know why?
X: What wagon train?
CALVADOS: Out by the lake.
CATLIN: No lake here.
CALVADOS: Out by the lake.
X: No lake here, I said.
CATLIN: Dried up.
STONE: You stay down here the night.
CALVADOS: And you come with us.
X: Why?
WANDER: Come with us or I shoot your hair off your head!

CUT

(*ESTHER sits in a subterranean room. She speaks to JANE and WANDER who stand above her looking down through an opening. The moon is visible behind them.*)

WANDER: Who are you?
ESTHER: There was a big black stink on the land, the red tide, dead crabs in the batter, dead records melting in the sun. Blue curd in the skyway instead of the clouds. Red stink everywhere. Clams open up, rotten sky, fish dead before born, chicken die in egg, a scrambled egg mush. Red tide. Dreams don't even go bad, they just die in their sleep, capsize

in unconscious. People can't sing no more, lose the note. Go off tune. Sand comes alive and rots no matter how it tries. Birds pungent in the air. Bulls with no ambition, don't fight in the ring. They love the death sword. Color blind to red. Pigeons fight with seagulls. Tide go out and never come back, rot out at sea. Die in scum and desolation. Beer fuzz on the water top. Everything become about nothing. Nothing has a meaning. Meanings mean nothing. Imagination stillborn. Keep on keepin' on can't keep goin' no more. Uncle Tom's Thumb caught in the door. Everyone look for trouble and find it without looking.

JANE: How poetic.

WANDER: You crazy girl.

ESTHER: I must be.

WANDER: Why you talk so weird?

ESTHER: What do you want from me?

JANE: Nothing.

ESTHER: Shall I show you my postcards?

CUT

(An elegantly set dining room. ESTHER and JANE sit at either ends of a large dining room table. CALVADOS,WANDER,CATLIN,STONE sit on the sides. All are elegantly dressed and eating soup. The top screen shows clouds in the sky.)

ESTHER: How old are you?

CALVADOS: Twenty five.

ESTHER: And how old are you?

JANE: Twenty five.

ESTHER: You are both twenty five.

WANDER: And I am too.

ESTHER: You are all twenty five.

WANDER: We are all twenty five including myself and I never lie about my age.

ESTHER: I have reason to believe you're all lying. Tumbling around in lies inside your heads.

JANE: Go feed the horse.

WANDER: Where's the gun?

ESTHER: Which gun?

JANE: We all have guns, how lovely.

CALVADOS: Did you visit the horse today?

STONE: I looked at him in the dark and his hands fell off and his face fell off before my very eyes but his eyes stayed in, rotting in their sockets without the benefit of a frame.

JANE: Heavens.

CALVADOS: Definitely not.

CATLIN: Morning yet?

JANE: It's the same old day coming over and over again.

STONE: It comes in different lights and weathers but it's really the same day.

JANE: It's alright.

ESTHER: It's not alright.

JANE: World without pain amen, world without end amen.

ESTHER: But you've come so far, covered so little ground.

CATLIN: But there is no horse, we shot it and buried it.

WANDER: Do you want to see the buried skeleton rotting?

STONE: Dig it up, dig it up.

CALVADOS: Why didn't you just let it go?

CATLIN: Because he'd find it and work it to death.

JANE: So we killed it, shot it right in the head.

WANDER: Now, no one can have him.

ESTHER: Slaughtered it.

CALVADOS: Of course you did, you shot it and murdered it and killed it and buried.

STONE: It was digging its own grave.

WANDER: And it jumped in to it anyway, head first and crippled itself into the grave.

CATLIN: And then we shot it, so it helped us kill itself.

STONE: We had one horse left and now we have none. None is better than one.

ESTHER: What will you do without the horse?

JANE: Nothing. It's dead and safe inside its tomb.

CALVADOS: It's better than being a bleeding leper parasite.

JANE: The light is getting less and less.

WANDER: How is the guy in the basement house?

ESTHER: Well, the candle light was devastating. His face corroded before my eyes. I told him I didn't want to see any light and to keep the room dark. I didn't want him to see me. I didn't want to see him but he did. He's restless.

JANE: To my mind, I don't think it was right. I just don't think it was right.

CATLIN: It just wasn't right.

WANDER: Where's the dog?

CALVADOS: Heaven help that dog without a bone because he will chew up everything in sight including you and that horse and the tree and the house and the chair.

WANDER: And heaven help us all.

STONE: Heaven help King Tut stuck away in that museum somewhere.

ESTHER: Your stupid archaeology.

STONE: Heaven help King Tut, I said.

CALVADOS: To hell with King Tut, why should be care about King Tut?

JANE: Anyway what did he ever do for us?

WANDER: A lot.

CATLIN: A lot of nothing.

CALVADOS: Plenty of nothing.

JANE: He had plenty of everything and now he's got plenty of nothing and now we've got plenty of nothing, so heaven help us not him, he don't need no help.

WANDER: Poor King Tut.

CALVADOS: You archaeologists are all the same. Who cares about that dried up old thing anyway? He's as crisp as a piece of shrapnel or pork rind, ain't nothing going to help him now, ain't no one can help him now.

CATLIN: So the hell with Tut.

JANE: He had such a wonderful future ahead of him.

ESTHER: And behind him.

WANDER: Now he's just all crispy and who cares ?

STONE: Poor thing, no one to feed him, to blow his nose, to wipe his ass.

WANDER: That dried out crispy nose.

ESTHER: Don't speak about the dead in such a way.

CALVADOS: Who gives a shit? He's dead.

JANE: Who in Sam Hill can help him now ?

CATLIN: Let the dead bury the dead.

CALVADOS: Pray for the dead and the dead will pray for themselves.

WANDER: They're so selfish.

STONE: To my mind, I don't think it was right. I just don't think it was right, it just wasn't right.

JANE: Who's that?

CATLIN: That man.

JANE: I hate strangers, send him away.

CALVADOS: There's no one there.

STONE: I told you there's no one there.

ESTHER: Yes?

CUT

(*Desert landscape. A distressed, raggedly dressed WANDER is running down a hill.*)
WANDER: Wait, wait a minute, I want to show you something! Wait a minute, I want to show you something!)

CUT

(*CALVADOS and ESTHER. CALVADOS scrubs the floor on her knees and ESTHER sits on the floor against a wall. The moon is visible.*)

CALVADOS: A sheep in wolves clothing.
ESTHER: I don't know...
CALVADOS: ...how this is to be constructed.
ESTHER: That's just the way it goes.
CALVADOS: I was taken from here and made prisoner once. And I was taken here and put here and stayed here. And made to stay here. And I don't know why but I stayed in here. And I stayed here and I stayed here for what seemed like a very long time. And it was a very long time, a very, very long time and it seemed like it was forever. And it probably was almost forever, almost. But then one day the door opened beautifully and I was let out, not miraculously. And I was let out and I went out. And I wanted to get out and get let out. And when I had gotten out, I didn't want to go anywhere. wanted to stay here. I mean, not in

here, but just here, around here. And not go home to where I had come from. And I couldn't even remember where I had come from. Or, I could eventually remember. But I realized that I had been here so long that all the people that I could remember were dead. Or if they were alive, they probably were so old that they couldn't remember me, but could remember me probably with sadness. But there was no way I could ever get back, because you see, in time, the geography between here and there had gotten farther and farther apart with time as the time had gotten farther and farther apart and so we were too far away from each other to make any difference. It wouldn't do any good. So I realized I just had to stay here and live with it. And so I'm staying here and I'm happy to stay here. One day that door opened and it filled up with light. And I went outside where everyone else was. And everything else just became a memory. And so that's it. Good night.

CUT

(*Return to the elegant dining room, blue dome on top screen.*)

ESTHER: Yes.
X: And what do you mean?
ESTHER: By what?
X: By showing me all those post cards?

ESTHER: Nothing, I just want to show you a picture of the outside so you don't get bored.

X: By what?

ESTHER: By me, by this in here. These four walls.

X: Six.

ESTHER: Six.

X: Well, I am bored and you can't un-bore me.

ESTHER: Then thank you.

X: And throw those pictures away before I burn them in the fire.

JANE: Go and feed the horses.

WANDER: The horse, the horse, the horses, I'm sick of those horses. I'm going to shoot them!

STONE: Then shoot them all!

WANDER: I hate this job!

JANE: I did not kill my baby.

CUT

(*CATLIN sits in a desert landscape.*)

CATLIN: First we lived here a long time and no one come by just us and horses for a real long time. Then Calvados and Stone came by here, run away from wagon train burning, so they stay. Me, Catlin. I come from out by the lake looking for a job. But we find out they really come because they like us. Then people say this is a leper colony. But horses don't get it, so we raise the horses. On day a car come by and Stone say he sure that girl Esther she scalped his friends and he puts her in the basement house. We don't believe it but time goes by and by and we start to believe it even though it's not true maybe. She try one night to come out of there and kill him. But I figure how many stories you going to believe? So she stay in there a real long time. And one day I take the lock off and no one notice. I tell her the lock is off but she don't come out. She stay in there in the dark, maybe you take her with you.

X: She don't want to go.

CATLIN: She got to go.

X: Why?

CATLIN: She ruined. She sit down there and play records all day and night, eat mushrooms. Every day Stone puts lock on door and I take it off. I throw the lock away and he finds a new one. Now she don't want to go, guilty or not. She sad, she sick, she happy down there.

X: Can't you convince her.

CATLIN: How?

X: Power of reason.

CATLIN: No reason, no power, no lock, no light, everything dark.

CUT

(*The inside of a rustic adobe stable, a straw roof above. Rain drops visible through the open doorway. All sitting or standing around the sides of*

*the room. STONE and CALVADOS puff on
cigarettes. The others crack pecans and eat them.)*
X: Where's my book? Where's my book?
Where is my book, I said.
STONE: Here it is, I burned it.
WANDER: Listen to the music.
X: It's shit music, you mandrill. I'd like to read
a book once in awhile, a history book. Where is
my Arabian horse?
WANDER: We shot it.
X: Why?
WANDER: We had to, it was lame.
ESTHER: Do you think I'm some Sad Eyed
Lady of the Lowland ? I will bury you.
STONE: Shall we play cards?
ESTHER: Alright.
STONE: Don't get so upset.
X: Why am I here?
ESTHER: Your turn.
X: I'd like to read a book once in awhile,
alright? Why do I have to stay in this bed?
STONE: You're sick.
X: What's the matter with me?
ESTHER: We don't know.
CALVADOS: That's why you have to stay in
the bed until we find out.
X: Where's the doctor?
JANE: He'll be here.
X: What's the matter with me? Why is this
happening to me?

ESTHER: Nothing is happening to you, you're playing cards.

X: I'm sick of this room.

JANE: I think it's rather nice in here, don't you?

CALVADOS: The light is beautiful in here.

X: There aren't any windows.

CATLIN: Yes, there are.

X: What's that bell ringing?

JANE: A false alarm, don't worry.

X: Where is my car?

ESTHER: In the garage.

CALVADOS: Don't worry about it.

STONE: Would you like some food?

CALVADOS: Would you like me to tell you where you are?

X: Yes, I did.

WANDER: I thought so.

JANE: Be calm, you're destroying yourself.

CALVADOS: Shall I tell you where you are?

X: Yes.

CALVADOS: Did you pass by a bridge on the way here?

X: Yes, I did.

JANE: Off the Corwell skyway in northern California.

X: But there's no snow.

CALVADOS: It's melted.

X: When I drove by the bridge it was snowing.

CATLIN: It's melted.

WANDER: But that's OK.

STONE: Can you breathe alright?

X: Yes. What are you playing?

JANE: Canasta.

CALVADOS: Spanish for basket.

X: Casket.

CATLIN: Oh, Jesus Christ.

X: Are my ears bleeding?

WANDER: Yes, a bit, but it'll go away.

STONE: Would you like some records to listen to?

X: Yes, please.

ESTHER: Would you like to see the horse now.

X: Yes , I've brought the money.

JANE: Would you like to ride it first?

X: Of course.

CALVADOS: What's the matter?

X: Who is that?

CATLIN: She's the cook.

WANDER: We're living here.

X: Who are those children in there?

STONE: They wandered here from the train wreck.

X: What language do they speak?

ESTHER: They don't speak at all.

X: Why?

JANE: We don't know.

CALVADOS: But they don't speak.

CATLIN: They won't speak.

WANDER: They won't because they don't.

X: Aren't you going to teach them?

STONE: We're trying.

X: Where is the pig boy?

ESTHER: Over by the lake.

JANE: Why do you call him that?

X: He smells like roses.

CALVADOS: I don't think so.

CATLIN: He's very smart.

X: How smart?

WANDER: He has all those horses trained.

X: Trained to what?

STONE: To run and jump and sing.

X: And what about the horse I want?

ESTHER: He trained it too.

X: To what?

JANE: To everything.

CALVADOS: That horse didn't know a thing when it was born.

X: And now it can read, I suppose.

CATLIN: Stop heaving.

X: What are you all doing here?

WANDER: We're all sort of bandits.

X: Bandits?

STONE: Horse traders, horse breeders.

ESTHER: That's why you came. For the horse.

JANE: Shall we go look at it?

X: Are you going to steal my money?

CALVADOS: We're going to take your money and give you the horse.

WANDER: Fair trade.

ESTHER: Fair trade.

STONE: We all live here together.

CATLIN: In sort of a truce.

X: Till when?

JANE: Till someone breaks it.

CALVADOS: Then all hell breaks loose and someone gets buried.

X: How often does that happen?

WANDER: Not too often.

X: When was the last time it happened?

ESTHER: A while ago.

X: How long a while ago?

STONE: Maybe last week, maybe last year.

CATLIN: Not too often.

X: Well, do you at least like each other?

JANE: Until hell breaks loose.

CALVADOS: And Cain and Abel start fighting.

WANDER: It starts up every once in awhile.

X: Good Samaritan come around ever at all?

ESTHER: Once in awhile.

STONE: They don't stay long.

X: Why not?

CATLIN: You'll have to ask them.

X: Who's that guy?

JANE: Piano player.

X: Don't talk much.

CALVADOS: Don't talk much.

WANDER: Just play piano.

ESTHER: Can't talk, just sing.

STONE: I cook, he sing.

CATLIN: He can recite the alphabet.

X: What's his name?

JANE: Red Sleeves, we call him Mangas.

CALVADOS: He was one of the casualties.

X: Of what?

WANDER: There was a boat sinking and he surfaced and swam ashore.

X: What boat?

ESTHER: Some boat.

X: Don't you have any answers to anything?

STONE: No.

X: How far is it to town?

CATLIN: Twenty miles.

X: How do you get food?

JANE: Grow it, steal it.

CALVADOS: Cook it.

WANDER: Kill it.

ESTHER: Skin it.

STONE: Cook it.

X: Why are you so desolated, dilapidated?

CATLIN: We're not.

JANE: Shall we go and look at the horse?

X: Yes. Do you like it here?

ESTHER: Listen to me, I'm trying to tell you something, a story.

X: Don't tell me any story.

ESTHER: I'm trying to tell you something.

X: What do you do out here?

STONE: Sing, read, work with the horses.

X: Is this a family?

CATLIN: No family, all our babies die.

JANE: We buried them all over here.

CALVADOS: They just born dead.

WANDER: They don't care to live.

ESTHER: They turn their back on the light.

STONE: Born with razor blades in their mouths, don't care to live.

CATLIN: They go live somewhere else.

JANE: Wander the last baby born here.

CALVADOS: But his and my baby died last year.

WANDER: And the year before.

ESTHER: And the year before.

STONE: So we stopped trying.

X: Any doctors come?

CATLIN: One came by once but they don't come anymore.

JANE: Said we have to go the hospital in the town.

CALVADOS: We don't want to do that.

X: Why not?

WANDER: They'll make us stay in there.

ESTHER: They took his sister last time. She never come back.

STONE: They said she died of complications.

X: Complications of what?

CATLIN: Don't know.

JANE: They buried her in the city and don't let us take her.

CALVADOS: Juanita had a baby last year.

WANDER: It died too.

X: Do the horse babies live?

ESTHER: They all live.

X: Dog babies?

STONE: Yes, that dog named Silvia had ten.
(*Begins writing on a scrap of torn paper.*)
CATLIN: They all ran away.
JANE: What's that?
X: Let me see that.
CALVADOS: What is this?
WANDER: I'm writing a letter.
ESTHER: What is that?
STONE: A letter.
X: This is not writing.
STONE: Yes, it is. I'm writing a letter.
X: To who?
STONE: To a relative in the city.
X: City of what?
STONE: City, the city, the big city, the nearest city.
X: What does it say?
STONE: None of your business.
X: How do you send it? Where's the mailbox?
STONE: No mailbox.
CATLIN: Wander goes into the city and mails it there. There's lots of mailboxes there.

CUT

(*CATLIN and JANE out in the desert. The wind blows violently.*)

CATLIN: Do you like the horse?
X: Yes. But keep away from me, all of you.
CATLIN: Why?

X: They keep showing me pictures of shrieking and killing. What's that?
CATLIN: Water. It's a bowl of tears.
JANE: Your tears.
X: Well, I don't want them.
JANE: Lay your body down, be calm.
X: How can I be calm when the world is spinning backwards?
JANE: I'm washing potatoes for God's sake, now get out of here!

(She throws a rock at the camera.)
CUT

(Four side screens go black. Top screen shows CALVADOS's face looking downwards. Above her in the distance is a blue domed ceiling .)

X: Who are you?
CALVADOS: An eye surgeon. I want to check your eyes.
X: For what?
CALVADOS: I might want to take your appendix out.
X: Out of my eye?
CALVADOS: Possibly, if we find it there.
X: And if we don't?
CALVADOS: We won't.
X: You're not an eye surgeon, get out. Get out of my room.

CALVADOS: What happened to your eye?
Once, when I was very young I had to do an
operation.
X: On who?
CALVADOS: On my eye surgeon teacher.
X: So what.
CALVADOS: So what? There was no one there
to operate and he had gotten a splinter of glass
in his eye and I had to take it out because no
one else was there so I had to take it out. And
so I tried to and I did everything he taught me.
He was sure I could do it and I was sure I
could do it and so I went ahead.
X: Go ahead.
CALVADOS: And I made a mistake. I cut the
left eye instead of the right eye and I blinded
him.
X: What does that have to do with your eye?
CALVADOS: I cut my own eye out and gave it
to him in the same operation, so he woke up
with another eye, my eye.
X: So what?
CALVADOS: That's why I have a patch.
X: It's very becoming.
CALVADOS: Thank you.
X: Do you enjoy being half blind?
CALVADOS: I actually can see clearer now.
X: What does that have to do with my
appendix? Two eyes are better than one.
CALVADOS: Not really, one eye is better than
two. One eye usually disagrees with the other

and they're always fighting among themselves and sometimes the argument gets violent and results in a myopic subversion between them that centers in the middle of the head. It becomes a cyclopean nightmare. It becomes encyclopedic and defeats the purpose of each individual eye. One eye wants to see one thing and the other wants to see the other and so they become of two minds and split down the center. They cannibalize each other and it's just not right.. They don't co-operate with each other. Does that seem right to you?

X: What do you want to do, cut my eye out ? Who told you all this?

CALVADOS: I discovered it myself. It's my own private idea.

X: Keep it. I cannot bear the sight of you.

CALVADOS: That's because one eye disagrees with the other. If you had only one you'd feel better about me. And which eye do you think is responsible for this discrepancy?

X: The left, I think.

CALVADOS: I think it's the right.

X: It really doesn't matter.

CALVADOS: I can't bear the sight of you. Get out of my room. I'll call the front desk.

X: Do you want to take my eye out? Is that it?

CALVADOS: One eye.

X: What if I give you your eye back?

CALVADOS: How is that?

X: Take my eye, put it into your own head and give me the patch.

CALVADOS: I think you'd better go look at the horse.

CUT

(*JANE alone in desert landscape, wind blowing.*)

X: Why don't you go into the town?

JANE: They can make it bad.

X: How can you make it bad?

JANE: You can make it seem bad.

X: But how?

JANE: How? By hating something. By hating it and hating it so much that everyone thinks it's bad. If you just hate it hard enough. Just by hating it and being sure you hate it hard enough so that other people hate it along with you, it usually works. You certainly don't get anywhere by not hating anything. They say you have to get things done by hating, that's the only way, the good and the bad.

X: Tell me about the horse.

JANE: Take it along and do that. Hate takes everything where ever you want it to go, or not go.

CUT

(*CATLIN sits on a horse. WANDER holds the rein.*)

CATLIN: It was born seven years ago. Its mother came with Esther. It was put in her

room and it had foaled a few months later.
Then Stone took it and shot it one day.

X: Why?

WANDER: He say they try and trample him in the field.

X: Did they?

CATLIN: No. And ever since he want to kill this horse because he say it's going to trample him again some day. Do you understand that?

X: Not really.

CATLIN: So, he say we have to sell it.

X: What about all the other horses you had?

CATLIN: Oh, we had a lot of other horses.

X: But what?

CATLIN: They all were shot or ran away because they were tired of eating grass and tree bark. Nothing else grows around here to feed a horse with too good but turnips.

X: But it looks healthy.

CATLIN: Oh, it's healthy because we feed it meat, it doesn't like anything else too much but that.

X: How could that be?

CATLIN: Oh, it'll eat grass and stuff but it likes meat, rabbits, some chicken.

X: What will I feed it?

CATLIN: Oh, anything, crust of bread and such. It don't need meat to live but it likes it. That's why Stone is afraid. He's afraid it'll eat him but it don't eat humans.

X: How do you know?

CATLIN: It never has.

WANDER: As it never will.

CATLIN: You'll see.

X: I don't want this horse.

CATLIN: But you have to take it.

WANDER: You want it, don't you?

X: I don't think so .

CATLIN: But why? It's great, wonderful.

X: It's such an ugly place.

WANDER: It's not so ugly here.

X: Yes, it is.

WANDER: But the horse don't jitter, it's pretty , don't get heartburn has beautiful teeth. You understand?

X: I don't want it. I'll have to leave.

WANDER: Because you think it's a leper colony.

X: Where did you get this horse?

CATLIN: I told you it was foaled here from Esther's horse.

X: And where did her horse come from?

CATLIN: It come from the best stock wild prairie horse.

WANDER: This no mulie, this ain't got no mule face, look at the face, face almost human, you see it likes you.

CATLIN: You have to take the horse.

X: I don't want to take the horse.

WANDER: You have to take the horse. He kill it if you don't take it.

X: No, he won't.

CATLIN: Yes, he will.

WANDER: He kill it and I kill you.

CATLIN: An eye for an eye, a horse for a horse.

WANDER: Lets go eat and not think about it for now. You're just scared but don't be.

CATLIN: It's a crazy light around here but that's nothing.

WANDER: You'll like the horse, you'll see.

CATLIN: And you'll take it with you and keep it.

WANDER: And then it won't get shot and buried here like the other ones.

CATLIN: Lets go eat. You're just tired.

WANDER: It's the chill factor. Bad chill factor in the air. It's a natural beauty you'll see.

X: Why is she down in that room ?

CATLIN: She like it down there.

X: She doesn't like it down there, it's all dirty.

WANDER: She didn't like it down there but now she does.

X: You shouldn't keep her down there.

CATLIN: That's not your business. Your business is to come get the horse. Not to worry about Esther.

X: Why don't you let her out?

WANDER: She won't leave, we tell her to go but she don't leave, she stay down there.

X: I can't believe that.

CATLIN: It's true.

X: Where would she go?

CATLIN: Where she come from.

WANDER: Nowhere in particular.

X: They said she came from the wagon train, Indians.

CATLIN: She might have.

WANDER: That's what Stone says.

CATLIN: But he don't know much.

X: She said she was driving her car and you dragged her out of it and stole her horse. Did you do that? Keep the room still, will ya? Did you do that?

WANDER: Are you really here for the horse or do you really think you're here to visit a leper colony.

X: But it isn't a leper colony is it?

WANDER: You tell us you're the doctor.

CATLIN: You're a doctor aren't you?

X: Yes.

CATLIN: Then stop looking at us so weird and tell us what you think.

X: I think that I'm here to buy that horse but I don't know who I'm buying it from.

WANDER: From me. I raised it and trained it.

X: Why do you want to sell it?

WANDER: I told you Stone will kill it if I don't sell it.

X: Why don't you ride it away?

CATLIN: He'll find us.

WANDER: I raised that horse from nothin' and it's my horse and it'll be yours.

X: If I want it.

WANDER: You want the horse. We look sick? Our skin look rotty to you?

X: Let me see your hand.

CATLIN: You see anything on it?

X: It might not be on it. It could be in it.

WANDER: If it's not on it, it's not in it.

X: That's not really true. Why don't you leave this place?

CATLIN: We don't want to, we like it.

X: You don't like it here, you all look at the sky weird.

WANDER: You don't like it so much here.

CATLIN: It's my home.

X: Why don t you leave?

WANDER: People in town say we can't leave cause we got rotty skin, they don't let us leave.

CATLIN: Every time we go to leave they bring us back.

X: I don't see any fence to keep you in.

WANDER: They keep us in.

CATLIN: Esther can't get out, we can't get out but the horse can get out.

X: What if I took you out?

WANDER: They stop you.

X: Stop me where?

CATLIN: On the road, they got people that watch for such things.

X: Then they watched me come in here and they'll watch me go out.

CATLIN: But they wont stop you.

WANDER: Cause you not crazy rotten like us.

X: But I could catch something.

CATLIN: They say it don't catch no more.

X: But it's extinct almost.

WANDER: We're some of the last and when we get extinguished that may be it.

X: Unless I walk out of here with it on me.

CATLIN: That's why you can't stay here too long.

X: Where is my car?

WANDER: We fix it.

X: Where's my car, I'm leaving.

M : No, you eat and stay and think about the horse for a few days.

X: I don't have a few days.

CATLIN: Yes, you do.

X: Why don't you come with me when I leave?

WANDER: They won't let us.

X: There isn't another town for miles, they won't know. What's the matter with her?

CATLIN: She act like a dog.

WANDER: Wild.

X: You put her in there, you made her like a dog. You act like a dog. Why do they call you pig boy?

WANDER: No one calls me that.

X: Yes, they do, I heard them.

CUT

(JANE and STONE sit on the dirt floor of a roofless abandoned building.)

JANE: She say we all crazy, she say we shoot and kill her.

STONE: She say we got leper skin, everyone think we sick.

X: But they come buy horses.

JANE: But they stay away.

STONE: They leave.

JANE: We sick. We look sick? Our skin rotty?

X: Yes.

JANE: But not Wander and not the girl.

STONE: No, his skin don't rot.

JANE: So we stay here, but Wander got to go if his skin don't catch the rot and Esther got to go, her skin don't rot and the horse got to go.

X: It's so dark down there no one can tell but I don't think so.

JANE: So you take Wander, you take the horse and you take Esther.

X: They sent Wander away, cut his hair and dressed him up to go to the city but he come back all sick, too weak.

JANE: But you can go but just know that you are ours.

X: Yours.

JANE: You ours, ours by right of conquest.

X: Why ?

JANE: You ours. Right of conquest. But you go but you be namesake for the horse. What your name?

CUT

- 282 -

(*WANDER and CALVADOS on a desert hill.*)

ESTHER: Shall I show you my postcards?
X: Sure.
WANDER: (*Holding up a series of postcards one after another. He holds each card next to his face as he describes it.*) This one is of someone killing someone but an angel comes down to save the guy. This one is about a bombed out place somewhere probably in a war it's burning up and the bomb probably looks like it was dropped from a plane or somewhere. This one is of a horse. I think it's a horse or a cow. I took it myself. Being strangled by a rope. And this one is from another war bombing. In this one you can see the whole city is wrecked but you can't see any dead people or anything like that. I think there's a cat there. And this one is of a lady being assassinated, they're going to chop her head off and you see everyone is crying. Those are her friends and there's someone trying to tell her not to be afraid but you can see she's nervous and she can't find the chopping block to put her head on but her friends are helping her out and the chopper guy is waiting. And this is one of someone drowning from a boat and sharks all around trying to eat the guy's guts out and they're trying to save him by stabbing the sharks with sticks

X: Do you think he gets saved?

WANDER: No, I don't. You never know what happens in the next moment of any of these pictures, if they get saved or chopped or what and this one is of a village somewhere on the sea and this one is of someone with a stab wound and an angel is saving him or telling him she's sorry. He could be dead already and that's why the angel is crying and this one is of the Beatles. This one is dead but the other ones don't know it yet.

X: Why are you showing me all these things?

WANDER: Because.

X: Because what?

WANDER: Just because I wanted you to see them. I though you'd like them.

X: Well I don't like them. I don't like them at all.

WANDER: So, then don't.

X: I won't.

WANDER: Why don't you like them?

X: They're ugly.

WANDER: Why are they ugly?

X: They just are.

WANDER: To you they are.

X: To anyone they are.

WANDER: They are not ugly.

X: You are ugly, they are ugly, that's all, and I don't want to see them. (*All screens go black.*)

WANDER: Look at them. Here, open your eyes, look at them.

X: No.

WANDER: Look at them, I said, and open your eyes.

X: You can't make me.

WANDER: Yes, I can.

X: No.

WANDER: I'll shoot you if you don't open your eyes.

X: Go ahead.

WANDER: I'll shoot.

X: Shoot. But I won't look at your ugly Beatle postcards of bombings, choppings and drownings.

CALVADOS: And here are some other postcards, look.

X: No.

CALVADOS: (*Screens return.*) Look, I'm going to show them to you anyway.

X: No.

CALVADOS: I'm going to anyway. (*She holds up the postcards to her face as she describes them.*)This one is of an old man looking at us and thinking "Oh, what an idiot we are."

X: You are.

CALVADOS: Looking at us and thinking what an idiot you are. And this one is of someone with a leaf or branch on their head as a decoration and I don't know what they're thinking and it says, I didn't write it…"Para la senorita Maria Martinez."

X: I thought you couldn't read.

CALVADOS: I can't but that's what it says. It has to say something.

X: It doesn't say that.

CALVADOS: Yes, it does.

WANDER: I can't read and it says "Greetings and bon voyage."

X: It does not.

WANDER: Yes, it does.

X: Shut up.

CALVADOS: And this one is of a girl looking at us and doesn't say anything. And this one is of someone with a scarf on their head and it also says Maria.

X: It does not.

CALVADOS: It says "greetings."

X: It does not.

WANDER: And this one is of the same girl and she's looking sideways in her red scarf.

CALVADOS: It's blue.

WANDER: And this one is of a room in the sky that's empty with nothing in it.

X: I don't care.

CALVADOS: And this one is of somewhere, a town by the sea with lots of rich buildings and churches.

X: I don't see one goddamn church in that picture.

WANDER: Well I do, they're all over the place.

(*Postcards begin to burn slowly.*)

CALVADOS: And this one is of an old man looking at us and wondering and thinking what an idiot you are.

X: We saw that one already.

CUT

(*Postcards burn throughout scene. They are gone by the end.*)

X: (*Voice over camera POV's wandering through desert.*)

Esther rode off on the horse but the horse come back.

So I stayed at that house for ten years or so. Took care of them as a doctor even though I swear to god they weren't sick. The horse died two years into the ten years and for the next eight years each one of the seven people died. Don't ask me what they died of. I stayed there for a year alone. Esther came back to get the horse and take it out of there but it was buried so we unburied it and she took the bones away in a bag. We shared the gun, so I gave it to her but tomorrow I go away. We could say they starved themselves to death but I would go into the town to get food but that town wouldn't give them much. Eventually they ate the horse and the only one happy was Stone because he was always afraid the horse would eat him. So he ate it happily but starved himself to death before the flesh was all gone. It made him sick.

CUT

(WANDER sits alone in a desert landscape.)

WANDER:....was pretty cloudy, geese going over. A fox barked at me at night. It rained all night. It's clear today. A tiny, fresh wind. Cranes are always flying over to the north but they way out of sight. I had a headache and a fever. My little horse is cowering and shaking. He's hungry. Today I shot a very small blue woodpecker. I took a small dish of water and a candle and pepper and some sand and the bird and boiled it. Then I made a cup of coffee with the rest of the water. It was the first time I eat in three day. I sewed my pants. There was a strong breeze all morning. I feel a little better today but I don't know where I'm supposed to go get food or anything. The birds are scarce and very shy and I'm weak and nervous. The wolves won't come close enough and if they did I'd be too nervous to take a good aim at them. I saw a few robins but they were too shy. But there's nothing out there. Wild birds fly over all night but they're to far away and it's too dark. I hope some of my friends will be out tomorrow. If not, that cameraman is lost and I'll probably follow. I just feel like I'm sinking in spite of all my philosophy. And I lost the gun. I hear songs on the radio but I don't know which way they come from and I lost the gun!

What is this shit?! (*Stares at the camera for 15 seconds in silence.*)

CUT

(*JANE and CATLIN,MANGAS in desert landscape, wind blowing strongly.*)

X: Where's the girl?

JANE: She run away.

X: Why she run away?

JANE: Now you stay here, we let her go off. She want to go, we let her go. You want to go, we let you go. But you take the horse.

X: I'll stay for a day.

JANE: No, you stay a day, you stay a long time, maybe forever.

CATLIN: We want you stay here. Maybe you can have a baby for us. You know, so we keep on keepin' on.

JANE: No more babies, babies finished here.

CUT

(*WANDER,STONE,CATLIN each on separate screen. ESTHER is on the top screen, CALVADOS and JANE are together on another. Each character stands at the top of an identical set of steps in front of the arch of a burned out building. They move down the steps simultaneously and approach the camera as the scene progresses.*)

CALVADOS: You gotta go now.

WANDER: No, I don't wanna go.

ESTHER: You like it here?

WANDER: It's my home.

STONE: This ain't no home.

JANE: It's a prison.

CATLIN: A leper colony.

CALVADOS: A horse farm.

ESTHER: A basement house.

STONE: You don't like it here.

JANE: You got to go out. Can't stay here no more.

CATLIN: You gotta go.

CALVADOS: You ain't sick. You gotta go before you get sick.

WANDER: Where I go?

ESTHER: Go out there. Just out. Out to the paradise land.

WANDER: I like the desert land.

STONE: Go, go out.

JANE: You got to go now.

WANDER: But why you cut my hair ?

CATLIN: We got to cut your hair. Make you look right.

WANDER: I don't look right ? I don't look right to you?

CALVADOS: You take the horse.

WANDER: The horse come back. You see.

ESTHER: You take the horse. You both go.

STONE: You both never come back.

JANE: You never come back. You see.

WANDER: I come back. You see.

CATLIN: You come back, you die here in the desert land.

WANDER: But why you cut my hair?

CALVADOS: We got to save your life.

WANDER: Life is a cannibal . It eats itself.

ESTHER: That's why you gotta go now. We fix you nice , you see. So they don't think you crazy rotten like us.

WANDER: But I like crazy rotten.

STONE: You go now.

JANE: Everything broken here.

CATLIN: You have to hurry up and get out now.

CALVADOS: You go now but you remember, you ours.

ESTHER: Ours by right of conquest.

STONE: Right.

WANDER: Right. By right of conquest

JANE: You go. You never come back.

CATLIN: You go and you go and if you find nothing then you walk on.

CALVADOS: A different direction until you find something .

ESTHER: You see a cameraman and you run. Don't let him see you.

STONE: But you don't stop.

JANE: You take the horse. It's a natural beauty. You'll see.

CATLIN: You see a pinhole and you run for it.

CALVADOS: If the horse don't fit through, you leave it behind.

ESTHER: Do you understand?

CUT

CATLIN: (*On all five screens wandering through the desert landscape from five different points of view. The five different takes of sound and picture play simultaneously and show her wandering off into the desert in different directions.*) I have a gun and we can share it. If I see someone I have a gun and we can share it. I have a gun and we can share it. I also have no water left but I have a gun and we can share it. I have a gun and we can share it, we can share it. Who needs water when you have a gun. With a gun you can get water. No one wants to share water but you can share a gun. I have a gun, we can share it. What can you get from water or with water? Nothing but I have a gun and we can share it. We can share the gun. Can't get anything with water but I have a gun. We can share it, we can share the gun. I have a gun, we can share it. But don't believe me. Don't. It never happened. This never happened, don't listen to me when I ask you to share the gun because we can't share a gun. How can you share a gun ? You can't you cant share a gun. I have a gun but we can't share it. We won't share it if we can't share it. We can't share the water if you have some. But don't believe me I'm not really saying this. I don't really mean this. So don't believe what I tell you I have a gun and we can share it because we can't share it. But I do have a gun and we can share it. I have a gun and we can share it. That's OK because we can share it. (*Sound and picture begin to fade into next scene* .) I have a gun and we can share it. Really don't believe me, don't believe a word of what I'm saying because I never said it. I never said it at all I never said it at all. That's all. We can share it OK? Alright. Greetings, bon voyage. What are you doing?

CUT

(*Five screens of wandering POV's in the desert.*)

X:... all he could do was puke but he ate it everyday. I didn't bury them, I burned them. Then I realized I was the only one there. There was no one left to remember me and if no one could remember me but that cameraman what good was that? I could wander in the desert for awhile or go up by the highway and hitch a ride so I did. But a car hit me and I lay by the road for a good long while and some wild dogs came. At first I thought they were coming to help me but I could feel them ripping my fingers off first and then I could feel myself being pulled apart. I tried to go back and find that leper colony again but I went back and nothing was there not a bone or ash or anything not a shred of evidence to the contrary or anything else. It didn't even look the same but I'm sure that's where it was. Not a thing, not a piece of anything. Not a suicide note from the horse, nothing. Nothing in triplicate. Not an autopsy, nothing. I don't think that air had ever been breathed and the light looked like it had never fallen on a thing in its life. But there was one fly. So I got on its back and rode it off, way up over the paradise land. Up where the light is, back through the pinhole. I come for a horse and I ride off on a fly. Back through the pinhole.(*Screens dissolve into to sky images*.) Up where that cameraman couldn't see straight, where he couldn't find me. (*Screens go to white*.)

END

Biographies

JOHN JESURUN is a writer, director and media artist based in New York. His presentations integrate elements of language, film, architectural space and media. His exploded narratives cover a wide range of themes and explore the relation of form to content. They challenge the experience of verbal, visual and intangible perceptions. His work is distinguished by his integrated creation of the text, direction, set and media design. Born in 1951 in Battle Creek, Michigan. B.F.A. Philadelphia College of Art/1972. M.F.A. in Sculpture from Yale University/1974. From 1976 to 1979 he served as a Television Content Analyst for CBS. From 1979 to 1982 he was Assistant to the producer for "The Dick Cavett Show" producing interviews with John and Mackenzie Phillips, Alberta Hunter, John Hammond Sr., Odetta and Tito Puente. In 1982 he began his theatrical career at the Pyramid Club on the Lower East Side with his groundbreaking serial play CHANG IN A VOID MOON, now in its 60th episode. (Bessie Award). Since 1984 he has written, directed and designed over 25 pieces including: the media trilogy of DEEP SLEEP (1986 Obie Award, Best Play),WHITE WATER and

BLACK MARIA, NUMBER MINUS ONE, DOG'S EYE VIEW, RED HOUSE, BARDO, PHILOKTETES, SHATTERHAND MASSACREE, SLIGHT, RETURN, EVERYTHING THAT RISES MUST CONVERGE, SEPTET,FIREFALL and SNOW. His company has toured extensively in Europe and the United States. His work has been produced and presented by numerous venues including La Mama, the Kitchen, the Walker Arts Center, On the Boards, Brooklyn Academy of Music, the Wexner Center, Kampnagel Theater, Prater Theater, National Theater of Mexico, Mickery Theater, Maubeuge Festival, De Singel, Theater am Turm, Granada Festival, Eurokaz Zagreb, Bogota International Festival,Vienna Festival,Kyoto Performing Arts Center and Spoleto USA. His short films have been shown at festivals and alternative spaces in Europe and the US. He is the recipient of numerous grants including fellowships from the Rockefeller Foundation, Guggenheim Foundation, National Endowment for the Arts, Foundation for Contemporary Arts, and the MacArthur Foundation. Others include the National Endowment for the Arts-Visual and Media Arts Fellowships,Asian Cultural Council, Rockefeller Multi-Arts Production BAM/Lucent Technologies Arts in Multimedia,MAP Fund. He has directed his work in Spanish,Japanese, Italian and German.

He has worked with various artists including Molissa Fenley, Steve Buscemi, Christian Marclay, John Kelly, Hideo Kanze, Neil Greenberg, Rebecca Moore, David Cale, René Pollesch, Fiona Templeton, Frank Maya, Martin Acosta, Barbez, and Ron Vawter. Directing credits include Roy Nathanson's Jazz Suite, "Fire at Keaton's", Harry Partch's opera "Delusion of the Fury" and music video for Jeff Buckley. He has taught at DASARTS/Amsterdam, Justus Liebig University, Goethe University, New York University,Tokyo University,Kyoto University of Art and Design, The New School and Bard College. His work is published by Performing Arts Journal,Ediciones El Milagro, Theater Communications Group, Sun and Moon Press, Yale Theater Magazine, Index, 2Wice, Felix, Theater der Zeit, Backstage Books.
Website: johnjesurun.googlepages.com
e-mail: shatterhand2@earthlink.net

FIONA TEMPLETON's work ranges across various disciplines. Her performance work is born of a conceptual investigation of theatre as a total medium – language, space, and time, and as an "art of relation", in particular in its thinking of the audience. It ranges in scale from solo to citywide works, and uses densely poetic innovative language. She has been awarded fellowships from the U.S. National

Endowment for the Arts in both Poetry and Visual Arts (new genres); an Abendzeitung Muenchen Sterne des Jahres for theatre; two fellowships from New York Foundation for the Arts for performance, & one for playwriting. She was 1996-7 Senior writer-in-residence at the English Faculty of Cambridge University, and 2000-2003 Arts and Humanities Research Board fellow with the Department of Theatre Studies, University of Lancaster. In 2002 she received the annual Foundation for Contemporary Performance Arts award for theatre. She is a Senior Lecturer at Brunel University. Born in Scotland, Fiona lives mostly in New York since the late 70s, writing and directing. Her award-winning and influential *YOU--The City*, "an intimate citywide play for an audience of one", has since been recreated in six countries and languages, including at the London International Festival of Theatre in 1989, and most recently as a key project of Rotterdam Cultural Capital of Europe 2001. There is also a film of the New York version. Her current project, *The Medead*, is an epic that retells the life-story of Medea, for 12 performers, to be produced by the Glasgow Tramway and the Rotterdamse Schouwburg, and has involved research into the origins of the Medea figure in what is now the Republic of Georgia. The full work will premiere in 2010.

NoPassport

NoPassport is a Pan-American theatre alliance & press devoted to live, virtual and print action, advocacy and change toward the fostering of cross-cultural diversity in the arts with an emphasis on the embrace of the hemispheric spirit in US Latina/o and Latin-American theatre-making.

NoPassport Press' Dreaming the Americas Series and Theatre & Performance PlayTexts Series promotes new writing for the stage, texts on theory and practice and theatrical translations.

www.ingramcontent.com/pod-product-compliance
Lightning Source LLC
Chambersburg PA
CBHW030346020726
47493CB00003B/716